More by the Author

Horror

Dissonance Junction

From the Shadows

The Dark Collective

Granny Bael

Anthologies

Unnerving: Volumes 1—3

The Mighty Pen

Tales of the Slug

THE DARK COLLECTIVE

LAUREN PATZER

BLUE FORGE PRESS
Port Orchard, Washington

To Joe McKinney

You were an inspiration to horror writers,
a stalwart student of the written word,
and a bright star in the darkness.
I fondly remember your kindness and generosity.
Rest in peace, my friend.

TABLE OF CONTENTS

THE DARK COLLECTIVE

LAUREN PATZER

INNER DEMON

I couldn't believe my luck. Here in the middle of an empty ballroom, I danced with a goddess. She smiled at me as we twirled around the room, her feet light on the ground like an angel flying through the air. Music gently tinkled in my ears like a symphonic music box, blades of metal popping into the air delivered their soft timbre as we danced through a doorway into a bedroom. I laid her down gently on a beautiful white cloud of lace and goose down, the soft covers embracing her like a lover. She smiled up at me, never saying a word. I pushed the folds of her delicate silk dress carefully out of the way and entered her, my manhood pulsing with excitement.

And then it ended. The ever-present demon in my mind chose the moment of ejaculation to bring my world tumbling down. Her smile and those beautiful eyes were replaced by the sickeningly real, crudely drawn shapes on duct tape wrapped around her head of matted hair and skin blackened by dried blood. I shuddered as I stepped off the bed, which revealed itself in the dusty air to be nothing more than a worn-out mattress with multiple springs jutting out like spears.

The lower half of her body was a bloody mess. I felt my gag reflex starting. I fought it back and shook my head. The blood drained out of my face as I realized the woman was actually a child. I ran to an open window and wretched. My fingernails broke on the windowsill as I clutched it with all my might and threw up until I thought I would pass out.

I looked around to get my bearings. I was in some kind of abandoned industrial complex. Weeds suffocated the decaying buildings in a thick blanket of green and auburn. The ground below the window was obscured by a brush so thick, it was probable my gastric expulsion still dripped down the tendrils of foliage, never reaching the ground. A cool breeze glided across my face, shocking me out of my daze. I numbly looked down and considered jumping. Couldn't guarantee I'd die though. The demon inside me would probably stop me as it had a dozen times before.

No more, I decided. I had to tell the police so they could stop the monster I'd become. I shouted into the dusty abandoned building. "No more!"

I woke in a clean hotel room. I sat up suddenly, looking around the room. I checked my body. I was in clean clothes. Perhaps it had all been a nightmare after all. But, I couldn't remember how I'd gotten to the hotel room. I didn't even know what city or state I was in. I reached for the television remote and, as I grabbed it, I saw the jagged edges of my fingernails where they'd broken off on the window sill. It hadn't been a dream, but a continuation of my living nightmare.

I flicked the television on and waited for a series of mindless commercials pushing products I'd never enjoy again to pass by. My stomach growled with hunger, but I didn't want to miss the evening news. I had to know where I was. I had to know what I'd done.

Station identification told me I was in Detroit. I blinked and tried to think of the abandoned building where the girl had met her death at my hands. I couldn't remember any street signs or billboards on the wall. There was nothing to tell me if I was still anywhere near the crime scene.

The evening news came on. A perky blonde described a fire at an abandoned industrial complex on the southeast side of town. The fire so intense, it had brought down the greater majority of the buildings there. Police suspected arson.

"No shit," I responded to the perky blonde. I started to shake a little then. Was that even a woman I was looking at? Maybe the mind fuck in my head was feeding me this line of bullshit while I watched a cartoon. I couldn't trust my own eyes anymore. When could I trust them before? How the demon put me in a fantasy world that I completely believed confounded me. I lost track of the weeks or months since I'd been living this fractured, hellish existence. Too many times to count, I woke up with a dead or dying body in my hands, sometimes on the cusp of a fantasy I somehow let myself believe. Maybe it was own subconscious trying to keep me sane. No, there was no way I was still sane. I had to keep away from people to keep them safe. It was the only thing I could do.

I looked at the phone. I could dial 911. Maybe the demon didn't know what that meant. Maybe I could get the police to come to me. I picked up the receiver and tried to punch in the numbers. In an instant I was across the room, looking at the inside of the closet. The phone was gone. I screamed in pain as I pulled the hot iron away from my ear and dropped it on the floor. I ran into the bathroom and splashed cold water on the burning side of my head. I cursed myself. I could have left the iron pressed to the side of my head until my brain boiled! Why did I drop it? What manner of man was I to allow self-preservation to ever be a consideration again? By the sink, the cold, glint of a straight razor beckoned me. If I was fast enough… I picked it up and pressed it against my wrist.

I drew in a sharp breath as ice cold rain dripped down my face, joining the pockets of icy dampness in my clothing. The dim light of a cloudy afternoon illuminated a festering alley in between some restaurants. A family of rats huddled underneath a dumpster, gnawing hungrily on the bits of food they'd dragged into their temporary shelter. I glanced at my right hand; it held a knife, dripping with blood and rain water. Across the alley, a homeless man looked at me with a bloodied face, eyes ripped out and ribbons of flesh dangled from the tortured sockets. He wasn't alive, of course, but I knew he could see me with or without eyes. His soul looked deep into my own and judged me for the murderous beast I had become. I noticed one of his eyeballs lying on the ground beneath my hand. I idly wondered if I'd used the knife to cut them out of his head or just ripped them out with my fingers.

Wait, I had a knife! I turned it on myself.

I stared at the cup of coffee in front of me. The waitress in the baby blue outfit smiled as she refilled it. I looked out the window of the restaurant and saw a billboard for the Indianapolis 500. Had I killed the homeless man in Detroit or Indianapolis? I had no idea. I picked up the coffee and drank it black. The bitter liquid burned slightly as it went down my throat. I ran my tongue over my teeth and picked bits of toast and bacon from them. There was a hint of egg there too. Evidently, I'd already eaten breakfast.

The waitress was a middle-aged woman. A little plump around the middle, but she had great legs. She brought the check and I stared at her legs. No! I turned away as quickly as I could, but it was too late.

I stared at the wall in the apartment. The faded yellow wallpaper with bluebonnets on it was spattered with blood. I looked down in my hand and saw the blood dripping from the broken off leg of a chair. I didn't want to turn around. Someone in the room behind me was dead; I just didn't know who yet. Perhaps I could just stand there until the police came. Surely they wouldn't miss my victim's body this time. I could only guess at the identity of the dead body or bodies that lay behind me. The crimes were escalating in their riskiness if not their severity. This was not a featureless alleyway or abandoned building; this was someone's home. I thought maybe I could just not move and they'd come. Take me away or shoot me dead. But, I knew the demon had other ideas. I had to know what I'd done before I blacked out again.

I turned slowly, seeing the blood spatter on the wall and the ceiling. Whatever had transpired had been a horrific beating. I imagined my clothes were likely covered in blood cast off as well, but I dare not look until I'd seen the totality of the crime. A body lay on the floor in front of the couch. I recognized the legs. I started to cry, knowing the poor waitress must've been complimented by the demon. She had no idea what she was dealing with. The poor, innocent woman was just trying to get by and thought she'd met Mister Right.

I shuffled slowly over to get a better look. Where her head had been was just a bloody pulp of gray matter and bone. I tried to remember what she looked like before. I couldn't. This is how I'd remember her forever. Unless... I ran full speed at the window, hoping I was several floors off the ground.

I landed in the lake, coming up for breath. The cool lake water on my bare skin chilled me. I looked up at a clear, blue sky. My attempts to kill myself to end this terror had failed again. I felt something touch my left arm. I swirled quickly around and saw the body floating face down in the water. All the heat left my body. I hadn't even gotten a brief interlude between killings. Here was victim number ten? Eleven?

Someone shouted from the shore. I looked over at the person waving wildly. I turned back to the body, confused. I quickly turned the body over and saw a beautiful blonde face. She wasn't breathing, but I couldn't perform CPR here. I grabbed her with one arm and then pulled her to shore.

The man on the shore was frantic. I calmly turned the girl on her back and began breathing resuscitation with intervals of chest compressions.

"Call 911!" I yelled at the man. He pulled out a cell phone and began dialing. The girl started to cough up some water and she turned her head so she could spit it out. Her blonde hair shone in the sunshine, giving her head a halo effect. She turned back to me and smiled. I smiled back. It was probably the first time I'd smiled in weeks... months... years? I didn't even know how long I'd been trapped in this personal hell. Now I'd saved someone's life?

I saw flashes of shared experiences over time. It may have been hours or even days, but I found my clothing changed. I spoke with her at length, and then I'd say good-bye. I should be running. How long before I would kill this one too, this angel? This breath of innocence in my darkened world would be extinguished, snuffed out through some horrible macabre method. Why was the demon torturing me so?

I tried to escape, only to find myself sitting in a cafe or greasy spoon where she would just be arriving to talk to me. I tried revealing my dark inner secrets, only to come back to the conversation moments later. Something else had transpired in the interim giving no hint at my dark internal nature. I felt myself drawn to her. The horror that I might actually care for someone and what the demon would do to them was too much to bear. I resolved I would end this nightmare before it turned worse. I couldn't stand to see her die at my hands.

Ellen. Her name was Ellen. She smiled and got up. I watched her leave through the glass doors, lined with streaks from multiple ineffectual cleanings. I watched her legs and smiled. Such beautiful legs. My smile faded away. The waitress flashed back to my mind. The prepubescent girl I had inexplicably slaughtered and danced with in the warehouse. Glimpses of other nameless deaths went off like flashbulbs in my cranium. No names, no other real details, just a timeless march of death and gore.

I stood up. I felt the pull of the demon as it tried to regain control. The light faded in and out, but I kept my focus and consciousness. I walked out the door into the sunlight. A street full of traffic swirled before me. Just a few steps into the careening metal boxes and I would truly know peace again.

The sky went dark and I stood on a sidewalk in a suburban neighborhood. The gun in my hand pointed directly at the face of my blonde angel, Ellen. Just in time, I pulled up on the gun and the bullet whizzed over her head.

"Run!" I yelled. I quickly pointed the gun at myself and tried to pull the trigger. It fought me. Something had changed, though. I was still trying and I wasn't blacking out. I watched Ellen run away screaming, my heart broken but relieved at the same time. Lights came on in the houses surrounding me and I was still there. The gun was pointed at my abdomen, but I knew that might not be enough if I managed to get a shot off. I forced the gun toward my head. It was like pulling a one-ton anchor through mud. I was on my knees, huffing with the effort. I finally brought the gun to my temple. The demon released me and I saw the details of all the crimes that had been done by my hand. Their names flashed briefly in recognition and I pulled the trigger.

I awoke strapped to a table in a dimly lit room. Grime caked the walls, marking years of neglect. I tried to move, but my body seemed to have lost all mobility. I could feel thin plastic straps on my arms, legs and abdomen holding me in place. The table was angled up so I could look straight ahead and at the sides by moving my eyes. My head pounded with a dull ache. The bullet had somehow entered my brain, but not killed me. Was I paralyzed? I could still feel.

"Paralytic agent," the voice said. It was Ellen. She walked into view, holding a scalpel in her hand. "When I realized I'd lost control of you, I jumped to the next nearest host. Your miraculous drowning victim snatched from the jaws of death. The girl you got to know. The one I wouldn't kill just yet. I wanted to see what would happen when you finally let down your guard and cared for someone again. I mean truly loved them. Now your true love will get to remember how she peeled the flesh off your body while you're still able to feel it, but not move."

She pressed the scalpel into my abdomen. I grunted involuntarily as the searing pain flared from the stab wound. Tears formed in my eyes, streaming down my face as the blood streamed from the wound in my side. Ellen left the scalpel embedded in my abdomen and walked over to a tray with a wide array of instruments stacked on it. I shuddered as I saw her pick up the cheese grater. This was going to hurt immeasurably.

I felt my finger twitch. The paralytic was wearing off, probably way faster than the demon anticipated. I wondered if it was possible my physiology had changed somehow with his infestation. I blinked. This was a good sign, but it meant I'd have to fake my way through the torture, not moving, not letting the demon know I wasn't under the influence of the paralytic. Had she somehow resisted him and given me a much smaller dose? I wasn't sure how I was able to move. I almost didn't want to. Death would be a welcome relief even if I had to endure pain like all of my victims had. Their deaths had been grisly. Did I deserve anything less? This wasn't about me anymore, though. Ellen was trapped with a demon in her skull, but how could I save her when I couldn't save myself?

She dropped the grater on the tray. She was resisting. This may be my only chance. Who knew how much longer she'd be able to resist? I remember my first days of fighting before I got worn down. It was perhaps the newness of the possession or perhaps a resilience of strength within the new host. For some reason, this was a delicate time for the demon. If I acted now, it might be the only time I could.

I couldn't give it my body as a viable host again though. A fatal injury that would take some time to kill me but had to have relatively immediate care would be best. Unfortunately, I wasn't a medical doctor or even a student of medicine. The demon hadn't shared knowledge of its keen ability to kill quickly or slowly. It just put me through the motions. I imagined a nice stab to the lower back would open up a bleed in a kidney and, while painful, I figured I would still be able to kill Ellen relatively quickly as well. I had to spare her months or years of torment at the whim of the demonic entity.

I maneuvered my fingers to grab the end of the scalpel and pried it from my abdominal cavity, adding to the wounds width all the while. It was not without its own pain, but on the plus side, it would help to ensure I died sooner rather than later. I glanced at Ellen. She struggled with picking up the grater; she still fought it. I raised my head up and looked at my right hand. The scalpel wasn't the best cutting instrument for this task, but the plastic zip ties holding me in place were much easier to cut than a leather strap or rope would have been.

I cut my right hand free and used it to quickly release my left. I paused, the scalpel at the ready. It was only a split second that I was able to consider my next action. I was taking a life, freely and willingly, to prevent a soul's torment. I could already feel myself weakening from the blood loss in my abdomen. Ellen finally turned, grater in hand and I lunged forward. I drove the scalpel deep into her chest, into her heart. She grabbed at the scalpel and fell to her knees. The cheese grater clattered to the floor; it was the only sound that accompanied the groaning gurgle coming from Ellen. Then she looked up at me and smiled.

"I knew it wouldn't take much to make you a killer."

"It doesn't matter. You can't make her a killer and you won't have me to play with anymore."

"But now, you're damned just like me," Ellen said. She fell forward and grabbed onto my leg. She looked up at me one last time and I knew it was Ellen and not the demon any more.

"Thank you," she whispered and then fell forward, lying on my shins for a few moments before she slid off onto the floor.

I closed my eyes and thought that damnation was worth saving her soul.

Then I heard the sound of Ellen dragging herself across the floor. I opened my eyes and saw her stand up. She looked at me and smiled.

"I gotta thank you, Frankie," Ellen said with drops of blood flying from her mouth with each word. "You were a tough customer, but I won the bet!"

Ellen raised her arms in triumph and then stumbled a bit.

"What?" I said with a groan.

"Dang, a dead body is hard to control. Better get this done before rigor mortis sets in. Then I just stumble around like a bull in a China shop." Ellen nodded and blood dripped from her lips.

I felt my consciousness slipping away. "What bet?"

"Oh yeah, hey Kataki! Get in here!"

A Japanese man walked into the room. He looked at Ellen and

then at me.

"Well, I'll be damned!" Kataki said.

They both laughed.

"It's a demon joke—get it?" Ellen shouted. A pudding like ooze dripped from Ellen's mouth.

"Oh, that coagulation is happening fast! So, anyway, Kataki, that's not his real name, which is actually more like a few screams, guttural groans and a sound like an ox farting, but I digress. He bet me I couldn't get an innocent to take a life. Lo and behold, I did."

"I killed all those people," I said struggling to keep my eyes open.

"Yeah, not so much," Ellen said as she stepped over to me and touched my forehead. "That's was all Kataki while you were set in sleep mode."

In my mind, the memories flooded back. I watched as Kataki or the demon controlling his body, slaughtered all those people.

"Why?"

"Well, it was just something to do, really," Ellen said. "After roaming the earth for millennia influencing corrupt people to do more horrible things, we kind of got bored. So, I bet Kataki that I could get you turned into a killer without you killing anyone. It was touch and go before I saw Ellen drowning in the lake. That's when it hit me—you had to care about someone's soul to really crack."

"Why did you pick me?"

"Oh no, that was me," Kataki said. "Had to make sure it was someone as close to incorruptible as possible."

"I just wanted to protect her," I said as the energy to hold myself up left me and I slumped.

"Oh, that could be a mitigating factor," Kataki said.

"What?" Ellen replied. "He killed her fair and square!"

"Not for the right reason. He wasn't really corrupted. I win."

"I'm going to agree to disagree."
"Two out of three?"
"Yeah, sure."
Mercifully, I died.

Ancestral Rights

She stood at the back of the church, silently watching the mourners pay their respects as they passed her coffin, a well meaning trail of ants following an emotional chemical trail. Some cried and some just shook their heads. Most were a bit dazed, still shocked at the sudden, violent death of their friend. She felt their sorrow and returned it. She would have cried, if she still had the ability to produce tears. Death transformed her into a creature of spirit, a being of pure emotion. The emotion flowing through her astral veins right now was sorrow with an undercurrent of bitter anger.

Her anger soon came to the surface. Her killer filed past the coffin with the other mourners. She wanted to reach out and strangle the life out of him, as he had done to her! She reached for things to throw at him, but her hands simply passed through the objects. She felt more anger as a disembodied soul than she ever felt when she was alive. The murderer paused briefly beside her coffin. He stared at her delicately painted face for a long moment. He bowed his head, placed a single white carnation on her dead body, and walked away from the coffin. At the door, he paused and looked back, his face gaunt and grim.

"Just one more and it will be done," he murmured.

She listened to the words with a sense of dread. Did he know where she hid her son? Her son was the only one left, the last in the blood line. Could he zero in on her son's location purely by sensing his blood?

She willed her ethereal form forward, floating out the door. She didn't have much time. As long as her killer was in town, there was danger to her son. She had to reach the cemetery where her body would be buried next to her ancestors.

Philippe Montreaux drove his steed hard down the west road of his sprawling French estate. His friend Armand Villanova followed close behind. Light drifts of snow floated across the road as the two flew down the road chasing their quarry, clouds of snow floating in the air behind them. Philippe caught a glimpse of another, riderless steed racing away from them. Philippe motioned to Armand to halt. They came to a stop beside a grove of trees.

"Gypsy's not on the horse. He's probably trying to lead us away from his true location." Philippe rested a moment, favoring his left, bandaged shoulder.

"Are you alright, Philippe? How much blood did you lose?" Armand asked. His own blood-caked wounds scarred his face, but the blood had frozen from the swift, cold ride. The heat of his exertion caused a wound on his neck to leak a light trickle of crimson.

"If we don't find him, does it really matter how much blood I lose?"

"No, I suppose not."

Philippe glanced around, looking for signs of tracks leading off the road. He caught a glimpse of vapor wafting up behind a boulder to the right.

"Damn, he's headed for the cave!" Philippe spurred his horse towards the boulder.

"What cave?" Armand shouted, springing his own steed into pursuit.

They rounded the boulder and looked around. Philippe hadn't been to the cave in many years. Finally, Philippe's eyes locked on a bush set against a small expanse of granite; it was dusted with a thin layer of flakes while the surrounding bushes were covered in snow.

"He went in there." Philippe pointed to the bush. It hid the bare outline of an opening in the granite.

"I'll go get help."

"No! We end it now, before he has a chance to prepare for a siege," Philippe said as he jumped down off his horse and walked to the opening.

"Damn." Armand jumped off and followed his friend. They disappeared behind the bush, knocking the last of the snow from the leaves.

Sunlight seeped in through fractures in the granite walls, dimly lighting the interior. Philippe and Armand entered the main cavern cautiously, swords drawn. They turned at a sound and were knocked down; someone grasped Philippe's injured shoulder and grabbed at Armand's neck. They squirmed away, but not before the gypsy got what he wanted.

Their eyes still trying to adjust to the lighting, Philippe and Armand stood back to back. From somewhere in the dark cavern, a voice echoed out in broken French.

"As you slaughtered my family, one of yours shall be cursed to slaughter the other!"

Philippe stabbed at the sound of the voice and felt the familiar resistance of sword sinking into flesh. A gurgle echoed throughout the cavern and the body fell at Philippe's feet.

"Your murderous, thieving band was hardly a family."

In the dark, it was hard to make out the body. Philippe grabbed it and dragged it out of the cave. Once in the light, Philippe and Armand gasped in horror as the gypsy's body decayed quickly into dust before their eyes. The two men ran back to their horses and rode back to the main house as quickly as their mounts could take them.

Weeks later, the last of Philippe's family fled France for distant regions in Northern Europe, their family hunted by Armand's.

Jacques Villanova gazed out the window at the falling leaves. Oranges, yellows, and browns whirled down an alley, given temporary life by a strong breeze. How he loved fall in the country. His hands suddenly gripped the musty taxi seat as a wave of memory overcame him.

His father lay on his death bed. White hairs fell from his balding, wrinkled head as his body shook with a violent cough. The old man's shriveled hand reached out to his teenage son.

"It's not so bad, son, to die with a clean conscience. Don't give in to the pain like Leon did. Fight the urge with all your might. It's the only way—" he shook again as the coughing took over and then fell silent, slumped against the pillow. Jacques closed the old man's eyes. He looked out the window at the falling leaves and cried.

Generations of Villanova men and women passed away violently fighting the insanity of the blood lust to hunt down the Montreaux family. All of them paid the ultimate price for fighting that urge— dead by 35, their bodies aging unnaturally from the curse. His father was only 33 when he died. But Uncle Leon lived to be 45, before he was sentenced to death by the State of Florida, ending a 14-year, 10-state serial killing spree. Uncle Leon almost wiped out the Montreaux blood line single-handed, nearly ending the curse on the Villanova family. He had returned to the United States to hunt down the last of them; before that, he'd 'cleansed' Europe and Asia of the Montreaux family line. He didn't live long enough to make it to his own state-imposed death sentence. The curse took him before he reached his first appeal; you can't continue selective genocide from a jail cell.

Jacques pulled out his wallet. He pried the faded leather apart and looked at the pictures of his daughter and son. One was 4, the other 6. They wouldn't feel the blood lust until puberty, the tearing at your gut, the wrenching and pounding of your heart as it struggles against the urge to hunt down the Montreaux family. For them, he would end this curse, sparing his children the pain and agony of fighting the curse. His children would be free. For the first time in 240 years, his family would be free forever.

The cab pulled up to the hotel. Jacques tipped the man generously. Material wealth wouldn't matter after tonight. Only death could buy their freedom, the death of the last living Montreaux. He reflected on how the second to last Montreaux tried to hide her son by putting him in the orphanage, but in the same town. How naive she was. How selfish. She wanted to see her child grow up. Instead, she'd given him his death sentence.

It had been a simple matter to break into the adoption records. Without them, it would've taken a little longer, but Jacques would've sensed where the boy was and eventually gotten to him. He felt the pull at his gut even now, pulling him down the street toward the boy's new home. The boy's blood screamed in Jacques mind. But he had to wait until dark, and then he could move freely. No one suspected him of any wrong doing; it would take months for the local police to tie him to the mother's death. He only needed a few more hours. A little rest would help take the edge off the pain.

He ran his hands through his 26-year old gray hair. Sounds of the woman dying echoed through his mind. As tears streamed down his face, he wished for the night to come quickly.

She floated through the cemetery glancing at the tombstones as she passed, searching for the sites of her relatives. Suddenly, she sensed something familiar—around the corner, a circle of tombstones—the Montreaux burial plot. She saw her own fresh grave was no longer empty. More time had passed than she thought. She'd missed her own burial.

A mist formed over the plot, twisting in the light breeze. It grew thicker, resisting the breeze. In the growing fog, she began to recognize faces. Her father and mother were there. Old relatives she never even knew formed next to them. She called out in joy.

"You're here! We must go, to save my son, your grandson, your great grandson, your—"

A ghostly hand grabbed her, pulling her towards the mist. She tried to resist, but didn't have enough control over her immaterial form. As she slipped inside the border of the mist, a soothing voice spoke to her.

"...we have to wait until the curse is broken..."

"No! My son will die!"

"...too much killing... make the sacrifice that others may live..." Dozens of voices joined together to make the pronouncement.

"No!"

She struggled to free herself from the mist until she felt her consciousness fading, as if she was drifting off to sleep.

From the silent shadows, they emerged—whispers of night, agents of darkness. The street lamps dimmed as they passed, even the moonlight was unable to penetrate the eerie, gray cloud. Wherever it went, silence followed; it was as if they consumed all of the evening's sounds in an attempt to fill a bottomless pit of hunger. All the nocturnal predators ceased their stalking, their hunger a poor comparison to the ancestral host that floated through their moonlit domain. Death was in the air.

A chill wind blew in from the north, rustling the trees, and whistling through the eaves of the New England houses lining the street. Shutters, left open to let in the fall breezes, banged and crashed in the sudden gusty wind. Trash can lids, abandoned toys, and various bits of debris clattered and rustled along the pavement. The sounds rang together like an orchestrated symphony to herald the arrival of the spectral entourage; but everywhere the darkness went, the symphony went silent.

Flashes of blue and silver erratically shone upon the ancient homes, reflections of the street lamps off of a child's forgotten pinwheel that bounced down the street, carried by the wind toward the ominous visitors. As it bounced into their midst, the reflections ceased, and the pinwheel stopped in midair, grabbed by an unseen hand. Slowly it rotated, suspended a few feet above the ground in the middle of the nearly opaque cloud. Then, as suddenly as it had been snatched from midair, it fell noiselessly to the ground. The air grew colder.

The silent band moved swiftly down the street, turning down a small side road. Seconds later, the ethereal company reached its destination. It hovered for a few moments above the lawn in front of the two-story house; toys and play things of the children who slept within were strewn haphazardly about the lawn. Slowly the cloud engulfed the small building. A momentary pause was all that was required for the cloud entity to sense that its quarry was not within the walls of the building. Peacefully, it returned to the lawn. The strange crew moved slowly down the road and paused in front of an old barn. The sentient fog made its way inside.

There on the floor of the barn, the body of a small boy laid, lifeless; the red marks around his neck revealed that he had been strangled to death. The silence was broken; a low wailing rose from the ghostly gathering. It grew in intensity, rattling the rafters of the old barn. With abrupt violence, the barn doors ripped off their hinges, and the cloud flew away from the barn faster than the strongest winds the small town had ever seen.

Back to the main street and then north, the now nearly transparent crew traveled, ripping up all the fences and greenery along their path like a targeted tornado.

Jacques sat on an old bridge that spanned a dry stream bed, celebrating the realization of a lifelong goal—the final destruction of the Montreaux family. Now he could rest, the last Montreaux descendant was no more. The pain was gone. There was no longer a pull towards anything. There was only peace. He looked at the hands that had strangled the life from the little boy and cried. A mixture of relief and remorse consumed him.

It took only a few seconds for the cloud to travel from the barn to the bridge. Jacques was violently yanked up into the air by the ancestral host. He opened his mouth and screamed a silent plea for pity. His body glowed for an instant, and then the cloud became luminescent with his life energy. His motionless corpse dropped to the ground.

Seconds later, the luminescence enshrouded the child's body in the barn. The small boy stirred and the light disappeared from the cloud. The boy gently floated through the air, sleeping peacefully. A few minutes later, the boy lay in his bed. The red marks faded from his neck.

A blue and silver pinwheel, tied to a bedpost with a ragged shoelace, rotated slowly in the cool breeze coming in through the open window. The window slid shut silently.

TO DREAM OF DEATH

A brilliant shaft of light pierced the dusty gloom in the basement as Paul shoved boxes off himself. He sat up dazed. He glanced around furtively for a clue to his whereabouts; there was nothing familiar. Sensing movement to his left, he jumped to his feet, preparing for an attack, but it didn't come. It was just a box settling. Reaching down, Paul felt the carved oak handle of his hunting knife protruding out of his boot; it was the only thing familiar to him where he had appeared. He crept slowly towards the door. Listening for any sounds on the other side, Paul inched the door open slowly, wincing with each creak of the dry hinges.

He dived quickly through the door, keeping an eye out for an attacker; but no one reached out of the shadows to halt his progress. Paul ran up the staircase and emerged in the kitchen, stumbling over a table and crashing to the floor. He recovered quickly and jumped into a defensive stance. Still, no one attacked. Paul looked around and saw nothing but a puddle of orange juice on the floor. Paul felt the cold juice soaking through his jeans and shuddered.

"This has got to be a Monday," he groaned.

Paul walked a little more quickly through the house, searching each room, not expecting to find anything. If anything had been in the house, he had frightened it away.

"Why can't it ever be in the first building?" Paul slammed his fist into the wall. The sharp pain cut through his frustration and brought him back to his senses. He walked out the front door.

On the hillside stretched out before him, tall, dry grass swayed in the light breeze. A column of dust rose on the road several hundred feet below him; a dark blue station wagon sped away down the hill. Paul broke out into a sprint down the road. He made it halfway down the hill by the time the car reached the bottom. It turned left; Paul paused to watch it gain speed and disappear down the interstate. He sat on the road, his head pounding from the exertion of sprinting down the hill.

"Never easy. Always hard! Why?!" Paul looked up to the sky waiting for an answer, knowing there wouldn't be one. Whoever graced the believers on Earth had abandoned him long ago. He was under the care of a much less hospitable entity now—one who enjoyed his suffering.

Three hours later, Paul hiked down the interstate. Normally, he could flag a car down, get a quick ride to his destination; but, there was nothing normal about the game. It kept the roads clear of all traffic, the landscape clear of all life, save plants and the 'other player.' When he finally reached the other player, the game would be over swiftly, one way or another.

Something lay in the road ahead. Paul glanced around, looking for signs of a trap; the landscape was depressingly clear of any. A trap would have signaled at least an increase in the pace of the game. Paul reached down and picked up the object. It was a beret. No, it was a flight cap for a flight attendant! Paul looked at the sign a few feet in front of him. It read 'Santa Rosa Airport 15 Miles;' he started jogging.

The Santa Rosa Airport parking lots were empty, except for a single dark blue station wagon parked in the center. The other player was not giving Paul a clue as to which entrance to the airport she had used, if she had even gone into the airport.

"She wouldn't have left the clue if she didn't want me to come here, and it would be easier to spring a trap inside the airport than out in the open." Paul walked swiftly to the nearest entrance, glancing around him briefly, just in case his logic was flawed.

The cool breeze of the air-conditioning was a pleasant change from the dusty heat outside the airport. It caused Paul to shudder from the cold as he was soaked with sweat. He walked a little softer now, partly from caution, and partly from the fact that his feet were blistered from the long jog to the airport. He strode swiftly through the airport, moving faster through large open areas where an ambush could not take place. He paused near the two rows of ticket counters, one on either side of the corridor. The airline symbols glowed in front of him like a taunting puzzle. He struggled to remember what symbol had been on the cap in the road; it resembled three of the ones before him. He would have to search them one by one.

He was searching the first one when he heard a noise across the corridor. Paul shot up and looked around; a single reservation tag floated to the floor in front of the counter directly opposite him. He caught the barest glimpse of movement out of the corner of his eye, two counters further down the corridor. Paul crept onto the Aztec tile, making his way quietly to the counter where he had seen the movement. He paused in front of the counter, unsure of how to approach. Finally, he decided an unusual attack held a better chance of success.

Paul jumped on top of the counter. A knife blade pierced his left thigh. A blonde flight attendant twisted the knife in his leg. Paul screamed in pain and then grabbed her arm to keep her from twisting the knife again. He used his other hand to shove his own knife into her throat. Shock passed over her face as she stiffened and fell to the floor. Paul slumped down on the top of the counter, listening to the last gurgling noises of the dying woman. When she fell silent, Paul laid his head down on the counter and passed out.

Paul woke up drenched with sweat. He grabbed his left leg and winced. His wife, Monica, stirred and turned over beside him.

"What's wrong, honey?" She looked up at him drowsily.

"Just a leg cramp," he replied, his voice cracking. He got up and started limping towards the bathroom. He drew in a deep breath as the pain in his feet nearly caused him to fall to the floor. The deep shag carpet was a welcome change from the pavement that had blistered his feet in the dream. He twisted the faucet on and splashed ice cold water on his face. The image in the mirror was gaunt; he hadn't slept well for the last week. The pain from the dreams was etched in his face; a pain no drugs could wipe away. There was only one way to stop the pain.

Paul sat quietly in the rented car, absently scratching the skin under the fake beard he wore. The radio played a Beach Boys song he'd heard four times today while sitting in the parking lot watching the winery trucks arrive and leave. The air inside the car was noticeably stale; he couldn't just sit much longer.

Across the parking lot, a blonde flight attendant stepped out of the terminal. She was in a hurry, struggling to keep all her luggage and paperwork together as she rushed across the parking lot. In her haste, she didn't see a crack in the cement and tripped over it, sending papers flying. Paul opened the car door and checked the lot for any possible witnesses. He grabbed a small briefcase from the passenger seat and walked slowly toward his quarry. She glanced up, startled. Paul set down his briefcase.

"Would you like some help, Miss?"

She breathed a sigh of relief.

"I just need to gather up all these papers," she said as she smiled up at him. Paul bent down and helped her retrieve the papers. After a few minutes, they gathered all the papers. She thanked him and walked away, heading for the dark blue station wagon Paul had been watching from his rental car. Paul reached into his overcoat, pulled out an eight-inch hunting knife, and shoved it into her neck at the base of her skull, angled upward into her brain. Her limp body slumped quietly to the ground. Paul reached into his coat and dropped a single red rose next to her body. He turned and headed for the elevator, leaving the knife with the carved oak handle protruding from the back of her neck. He picked up his briefcase on the way.

As he walked between the cars, Paul removed the snug transparent silicone gloves and placed them inside the briefcase. When he reached the terminal, Paul strolled to one of the valets and handed him the briefcase; he asked the valet to check it for the 5 P.M. flight to Mexico City. The valet's white gloves accidentally wiped all traces of Paul's brief contact with the briefcase. Paul walked into the terminal, watched the valet pass by him, and then stepped into the bathroom. He removed the beard, dropped it into the toilet and flushed. He took off his overcoat, left the bathroom, and headed for the bus stop. He caught the bus headed inland. He dumped the overcoat in a restaurant dumpster in the city.

Four months passed before Paul started getting dreams again. He held out for nearly five weeks before seeking a doctor's help for the pain. They couldn't locate the source, but gave him some pain killers to help stop the pain. A week later, a female lawyer was brutally slain in a mall bathroom four states away; a single rose was laid next to the victim. Paul called the doctor to thank him for the pills; they were starting to work.

35

Agent Travis looked at the mess before him. There was no rhyme or reason to the file laid out across his desk—fifteen people slain in the past four years. A single rose was left next to the victims; but, there were no other connections. Most of the crimes weren't even in the same state. Abandoned rental vehicles and garbled physical descriptions of a suspect, male of varying height were the only correlations between the cases. Whoever it was knew how to disguise himself, but his victim choice followed no discernible pattern. He could strike anyone, anywhere and he had, at least fifteen times. Fortunately, the press hadn't caught on to it yet. That would've complicated the matters with copycat killers.

Agent Milton walked into Dean Travis' office with a smile on his face. "We've got a break, Dean. Not a big one, but something."

"The Doppelganger?"

"I think so. L.A. office got a call from one of the airlines operating out of Sonoma. An abandoned briefcase, flown to Mexico City the day of Vanessa Miken's murder, it was checked in by one of the valet's. We got a physical description, but it could be just as faulty as the rest of them."

"What was in the bag, Blake?"

Blake Milton smiled. "Fingerprints on the handle were smudged beyond recovery, but there was a pair of gloves in the case. We got DNA from Doppelganger inside the gloves. Blood trace from the victim and a rose thorn on the outside of the case. If we can catch him, we've got that much towards a conviction."

"DNA give us any leads?"

"White Caucasian male. No match in the national database."

Dean reached for his coffee. "So, that narrows it down to a few hundred million white Caucasian males between 18 and 80 that we don't have on file. This male must have access to public places and know how to use public transportation. We should have him by the end of the week!"

"If it was simple, Dean, we'd have caught him already. What's maddening is that he doesn't fit a profile. If he had to kill to feed his urge, he'd be killing more often. His victims range from a fifteen year old boy to an eighty year old woman. There's no pattern to his attacks, other than the fact that they're completely random. No prolonging the victim's death, or torture, and he doesn't kill them all in the same way. Nothing in common except for the rose."

"There were two attacks in Philly."

"Two years apart. No other cities repeated. He's not doing this based on convenience of location."

"And, even though it was only used in two of the murders, there's the knife."

"From a mail-order company in China that doesn't want to cooperate with a foreign investigation."

Dean sat up in his chair and grinned. "Maybe they don't have to cooperate. Get me all the mailing lists for weapons magazines and related mailings."

"What d'ya got in mind?"

"Cross-reference the list with our database."

"He's not in our database." Blake paused then a smirk crossed his face. "So, you'll eliminate everyone in the database and find out whose left."

Dean smiled. "At least, it's a start. You catch on quick, Blake."

A cool breeze rustled the palm leaves over Paul's head. The bright sun glared down at him, forcing him to cover his eyes. He reached for his drink, pausing to caress his wife's back as she lay sunbathing. He raised the glass to his lips and sighed. The toothpick umbrella in the drink tickled his nose.

"Nice vacation. All I really needed was a nice vacation."

Monica turned over and sat up. Paul relaxed on the lawn chair, his hand resting comfortably on the glass. His hand moved down the glass and came to rest on a familiar surface. Paul frowned at the feeling; he didn't remember bringing a baseball bat with him. He looked at Monica as she raised her hand; something glinted in the sunlight. With one swift motion, Monica brought the knife down, driving it deep into Paul's abdomen.

"No!" Paul screamed striking her with the bat before the pain reached him. The sickening crack as her skull broke open reached his ears just before the incessant thudding of his heart beat marked the steady passage of blood flowing from his abdomen. He doubled over as she fell onto her chair; a trickle of blood dripped to the sand beneath her. Paul winced as he watched the drops fall noiselessly to the sand and then he passed out.

Paul jumped out of bed, cursing and clutching his stomach. Monica sat up, pulling the satin sheets up around her.

"Paul, what's the matter? What's wrong?"

Paul looked at her, shaking his head, trying to clear the dizziness and disorientation. His eyes fixed on the fox skin on the wall above the dresser; he couldn't focus.

"Got bad cramps... think I'm gonna be sick..."

Paul stumbled to the bathroom and threw up in the toilet. His face was pale. The one dream he dreaded ever having; the pain wrenching his stomach was nothing compared to the pain in his heart. He gripped the bowl as the next wave of spasms wracked his body. He wondered if he was brave enough for suicide.

Dean frowned.

"I'm sorry, Blake, but this is where your theory breaks down. He doesn't need that much income. His travels in these cases could amount to a bill of maybe two or three thousand a year. I could handle that much for traveling expenses a year. A cruise for me and my wife costs that much. He used stolen cards for the rental cars; cards stolen from the local area, no less. You want me to narrow the scope down to… everyone we have on the mailing list, basically."

The phone interrupted Dean's assault. He listened for a moment and then put down the phone, shaking his head in disbelief.

"We got an anonymous tip on Doppelganger."

They rushed out of the office.

Only a little while longer, Paul mused, and it'll be all over. He was in so much pain he could hardly stand. He slumped in the chair, smoking a cigarette, praying for the clock to move faster. The sound of a door opening caused him to sit up in shock.

Paul's hands started shaking. He didn't know if he could hold himself off long enough. She would be out of danger if she wasn't here. A couple more hours, maybe less, and it would be over.

"Hey, honey." Monica smiled as she walked to him. His hands fumbled with the cigarette. "Geez, you look like hell. You should get some rest."

"Get out."

Monica looked dazed for a moment. She backed away from him. "Paul, what's wrong?"

Paul stood up and looked at his love, standing in the doorway. "Get out now before I kill you."

Monica smiled. "Paul, you poor thing. I'm not going to leave you now; I've put too much into this relationship."

"I don't love you," Paul lied, regretting the words as they left his lips.

"I'm not talking about love, Paul. I'm talking about time and energy; it's taken so much to drive you to the brink. I'm not going to leave now, just when you're on the verge of going completely insane."

"What?" Paul staggered towards her. She smiled at him; it was the same cruel, twisted smile he'd seen in his dreams in the game on the face of every one of his attackers.

"Who do you think has been putting those dreams into your head?"

Paul shook his head. He must be hallucinating. "No, you can't be. Get out."

"Don't tell me the hunter is beaten so easily, Paul, darling." The words dripped icily from her lips. Her voice was the same voice of all his opponents in the dreams. Evil. Deadly.

"Why...how...?" Paul shook his head again. Could this be real? Was this reality or another dream?

"The boy in Fremont. The one you killed with the hammer. I sent him to you in the dreams. You remember the old lady in Halifax? How funny that you felt threatened by her; what was she, eighty-five or something?"

"No... I can't..."

"How does it feel to hunt your own kind, Paul? Does it give you the same satisfaction as slaughtering a deer in the forest or blasting a raccoon from its huddled perch in the branches of an oak tree?"

Monica walked slowly around the living room, pointing out hunting trophies and awards as she talked. She made a circle coming back towards his haggard form leaning on the door jamb.

"Was the stalking of your human victims as exciting and thrilling as stalking and killing the majestic arctic wolf? Is cutting a woman's throat anywhere near as enthralling as skinning your latest bag in the hunt?"

Paul slapped her as hard as he could, knocking her across the living room. Monica caught herself on the recliner before she hit the wall. She laughed.

"Look at the walls around you, Paul; chock full of your sport. The fox skin in the bedroom, the mule deer gracing the hearth over the fireplace. The only thing missing is the skins of your human prey. Just think of me as nature's revenge, Paul; doing what nature can't. I've had so much fun watching you suffer. I wondered why you didn't have the same remorse over the animals you slaughtered. Your anguish over the loss of human life has been exquisite; I've really enjoyed it. You were much more effective, cunning, and inventive than the last hunter. It's too bad you slipped up."

"What?" Paul stumbled into the living room after her.

"The briefcase in Mexico City. You remember right after you slammed that knife into the stewardess' head? The airlines gave the FBI the briefcase. It's only a matter of time. But don't worry Paul; I'll be here with you to the end."

"Yes, you will." Paul strode as quickly as he could into the bedroom, adrenaline fueling his every move, clearing the haze in his mind. He didn't have much time left. He rummaged through the top shelf in the closet and found the knife; it was identical to the one he'd used in Santa Rosa. When he returned, Monica was at the front door.

"No, you're not going to escape!" Monica ran from the door to the other side of the living room.

"I'll kill you like I killed the others!"

"Help! Somebody, help me!" Monica screamed as Paul raised the knife.

The door flew open. Three FBI agents stormed into the room, guns drawn. "Freeze, FBI! Drop your weapon!"

Paul turned to look at them. His jaw dropped. "No!" He turned to stab Monica and the agents fired. He dropped the knife as he fell on top of Monica. His life hadn't quite slipped away when she whispered in his ear.

"Guess the hunter lost the game this time. Again."

The agents lifted Paul off Monica; she got up and buried her head in Blake's shoulders. Dean checked Paul's vital signs and shook his head.

"He was a damned international banker. He had plenty of opportunity to move about whenever he wanted. However, he didn't get into the country until about three years ago. His passports don't show him entering the U.S. when the previous years of murders were done." Blake plopped the file on Dean's desk.

"Pretty strange, all right."

"Maybe we can get some answers from his wife."

Dean shook his head. "That's stranger still. She's gone. Disappeared. We checked on her and found nothing. As far as the U.S. government is concerned, she never existed. Never held a job, was never born, so on, so forth."

"Witness Protection Program?"

"No. I mean she never existed. We have her name from the statement she gave us. According to her, they married in Vegas two years ago."

"If we can find her, maybe she can shed more light on his whereabouts."

"I don't have any real reason to look for her; case is closed. Let's drop it. We got the killer and solid evidence from his apartment linking him to the murders over the last two years. I know the bureau isn't going to want to keep this one open. Let's call it a week."

"He would've been stopped by this time anyway."

"What are you talking about?"

"He had a lethal amount of tranquilizers in his stomach according to the autopsy. He was committing suicide. There was even a note inside his night stand confessing to the crimes.”

“So he called and turned himself in?”

“No. It was a female voice. The note was typed, but not signed.”

The man walked through the crowded lodge to the bar. Hunting trophies lined the walls; every local animal had a stuffed head hanging there. After several minutes, he reached the bar, ordered a drink, and found a bar stool.

A beautiful blonde approached from across the bar. She seemed to grimace at the trophies on the wall. She was also a hunter; however, her chosen prey had just seated himself at the bar. She took the seat next to him and ordered a drink.

“Hi. Are you new around here?” The man said, sitting a bit taller.

The blonde smiled. His mind was completely open to her; he’d make a fine hunter/victim.

“Yeah. I’m Monica. Want to have some fun?”

THE GLOVE

Alan stared at the mitt, expecting it to glow or jump from the table. It laid still as the air on a stale summer night. It appeared to be a perfectly normal but well used leather glove, the faded cowhide nearly worn through in places, the stitching loose but sturdy. Alan detected a stain of red dirt on the tip of the pocket where it had scraped the ground so many times after a grounder the hide was permanently marked. There was nothing abnormal about its appearance. It was just an old baseball glove.

The auction site listed the former owner as Art Donovan, three time golden glove winner and notorious serial killer. If it hadn't been for his successful run in the big leagues for five years, there was some doubt as to whether or not his five-state killing spree would've been that notable. There were plenty of murderers in the world. Serial killers were disturbingly common, but they were not all famous. To have a baseball player at the height of his career simultaneously slaughtering a dozen people over the span of his career, that was notable. In fact, it was downright legendary.

The baseball career on its own was one for the record books. Art had an amazing ability to snag fly balls magically out of the air like they were on a string attached to his glove. Defensively, Art was unmatched in the league. Offensively, his performance varied on how recently he'd been seen on the sidelines obsessively caressing his glove like a rabbit's foot, trying to rub the luck into his hands before he placed them on the bat. People called it a superstitious ritual; it was all in Art's head. He had the ability but he psyched himself out if he didn't have a pawing session with his mitt right before facing the pitcher. No one on his team called him on it since his ritual seemed to work. The opposing players gave him an earful whenever they got the chance.

Halfway through the first season that Art played, he wowed them in the stands. It was also when the first body was discovered. The head of the victim had been smashed beyond recognition with what appeared to be a baseball bat. The damage was so bad, even dental records were useless in identifying the body. A DNA trace matched a serviceman's file and they finally discovered the body belonged to a rival teammate in the minors that had gone missing weeks earlier. At the time, the link between Art and the victim was tenuous at best. There were dozens of more likely suspects.

The fan in Philadelphia that expired with a baseball shoved in their mouth just before the end of the season gave everyone the shivers. Was this the same fan thrown out of a game for tossing things from the seats at Art Donovan? Again, it was a coincidence. Baseball seemed to tie the two victims together, but not in a meaningful way to Art Donovan. It still left many other suspects interconnected to the case.

Art's second season was unremarkable. His performance on the field suffered. His team gave him a hard time. His fans turned on him. It was sad to see a player go from shining star to has-been in a single year. Also absent was Donovan's ever present mitt. People wondered if he had lost his lucky charm and it was messing with his head. The volume of dead bodies associated with Art Donovan was just as scarce as his glove. No hits for Donovan on or off the field.

Succumbing to the pressure, Donovan listened to his coach and returned the third season with the ragged glove in hand. The body count didn't seem to increase as far as anyone noticed. The third season flew by and Donovan was at the top of his game again. All Star, MVP, and Golden Glove—he won all the accolades a player could. It all seemed so perfect. Maybe it was the glare of the spotlight that was his final undoing.

It was mid-fourth season when police uncovered the killing field, the burial ground with half a dozen victims in Donovan's hometown. Someone had noticed wild dogs gathering in an overgrown field and called out a posse to hunt them down, concerned about their own livestock. One of the hunter's stumbled on the remains that had been dug up by the wild animals. A woman who worked the concession stands in a stadium three states over had gone missing in the middle of the third season of Donovan's career, when he was at the height of his game. She'd gone missing right after a startling performance by Donovan on the field, ushering his team into their tenth win in a row. Dangling around the neck of her decaying body was a baseball jersey used to strangle the life out of her. It wasn't Donovan's jersey, but it was one of his teammates. The teammate had reported the jersey missing after the game. That put the teammate in the headlights as suspect number one.

One of the other victims had been killed with a souvenir pen shoved into their brain through the right eye socket. Another had been bludgeoned to death with the metal cleats of a baseball shoe. A field rake, ball bag, and other baseball related paraphernalia featured prominently in the other deaths. Someone was killing people with a baseball theme and they were doing it a lot.

It wasn't until near the end of Donovan's fifth season that police were able to track down his old equipment, sold to collectors and containing trace amounts of the victims' blood and DNA on all of them. Donovan finished out his season before he was charged. He claimed he was being framed. When confronted by the evidence and some of it indisputably linked to him and only him, he broke down and blamed it all on the glove. The cursed glove had been passed to him for a high price from a medicine man in New Orleans. Sticking to his story gave him the insanity defense and he managed to convince a jury. That's why Donovan was still alive.

The state auctioned off everything related to the case, the proceeds going into a victims' fund. The morbidly curious greedily bid on objects of death. That was how Alan had happened upon the glove. He was a big fan of Art Donovan growing up. Now that he was about to enter college on a baseball scholarship, he spent a large portion of the money he'd saved up for college on his idol's single most famous possession: the cursed glove.

Alan picked up the glove and turned it around in his hand. He didn't notice any distinguishing marks up close. He wondered briefly if it was even the famous glove. Maybe the certificate of authenticity had been faked. The soft, worn leather under his fingers felt warm and comfortable. He mused this is the nicest glove he'd ever laid his hands on before. He brought it to his nose and sniffed the old leather, smelling of baseball and popcorn from the years of wear and stadiums it had seen.

It wasn't until he slid it on that Alan knew this was a special glove. He knew he would do great things with it, break records, and wow the college scouts. His big league aspirations weren't even a full college career away!

First, though, he had to get rid of that pesky player from Wisconsin who was vying for his spot on the squad. That 'nobody' thought he could compete with Alan? A swift bat to the head would keep him from ever competing again.

DROWNED SECRETS

The rain poured down on the roof, the vibrant thrum of drops impacting the roof added a constant level of sound to the conversation inside the house.

Butch Seller sat on the sofa; his hands ran through his soaking wet hair. Two police officers stood by him. One took notes on a notepad while the other did the questioning. The rain outside came down hard.

"She loved that dog so much," Butch said as he stared at the coffee table.

"You say she had the dog on a leash?" the questioning officer asked as he glanced around the room, looking for any tell tale signs of a struggle. The room appeared immaculate, nothing out of place.

"She was always very careful," Butch replied, nodding his head. "I don't know, maybe the rain made the leash slick and it slipped out of her hands."

In his mind, Butch relived the events of the evening silently, enjoying them. Butch dragged a dead dog on a leash behind him. The weight of the thing caused his muscles to strain. He enjoyed the heft of the thing as he walked to the edge of the bayou, swung the dog on the end of the leash to get momentum and tossed the dog and leash into the swollen rushing waters.

Butch stood up, agitated by the narrative he fed the officers.

"When the dog slipped into the bayou, she called to me. I went out and saw her going over the edge toward the water. I guess she was trying to get Fifi."

"The dog's name was Fifi?"

"Yeah, I didn't name it. It was a full-size poodle mixed with something else. She really loved that dog."

"What happened next?"

"I ran over to the edge of the bayou and, Oh God, that's when I saw her slip in and get caught up in the water. It happened so fast and then she disappeared under the water. That's when I called 911."

The scene played out differently in Butch's mind. Butch wore gloves as he dragged Melinda's body to the edge of the swollen bayou and rolled it into the water. A car drove by, catching Butch in its headlights. Butch ran to the house.

The questioning officer walked around the living room and looked at the pictures on the wall.

"You and the missus have any marriage troubles?"

The memory of Butch wearing gloves as he punched Melinda in the jaw, knocking her unconscious doesn't seem to disturb him. He remembered getting a small thrill as he heard her body hit the floor.

Butch shook his head.

"No. We just celebrated our tenth anniversary, for God's sake."

Butch blinked away the tears as they formed. He was deliriously happy she was finally gone. Ten years of her droning on and on, and he was finally rid of her. The burden it had lifted off his mind!

"I wish I'd never gotten her that dog!"

"I'm sorry, Mister Sellers. These are just standard questions we're required to ask."

Butch nodded. The memory of him snapping the dog's neck

seemed to give him more comfort than the officer's words.

"I understand, Officer."

The officer stopped in front of the fireplace. He looked in and noticed a lot of ashes. He took a poker and stirred the ashes. Red embers reveal themselves amidst the dusty carbon flakes.

"Did you have a fire going tonight?"

"Yes. We always light one when it's storming out, in case the electricity goes out."

Butch stared at the fireplace as the memory of him standing there earlier played in his mind. He stood in front of the fireplace with a crackling fire going and tossed the gloves in. He smiled and stared at the flames. In his hand, the phone had a nine, one and one entered with his thumb poised above the Call button.

The officer put the poker back and walked in front of Butch.

"We're sorry for your loss, Mister Sellers. We're doing everything in our power to find your wife."

Butch nodded and wiped away the tears.

"Thank you."

The two officers walked out and Butch sighed.

That evening, Butch tossed and turned in bed as he tried to sleep. His mind somehow wouldn't let the murder of his wife go completely unpunished.

Butch is trapped by thick mud along the shore as he stared in horror at the brown, milky bayou water surface suddenly broken by Melinda bursting out of the water, covered in weeds and mud.

Butch jerked awake. He blinked into the darkness. He shook his head and laughed.

"She's swept into the ocean by now along with that stupid mutt."

He lay down and closed his eyes.

"Maybe a gator ate them," he whispered happily as he snuggled the pillow contentedly.

The sound of a dog growling caused him to sit up. He looked quickly around the room.

"Fifi?" Butch whispered, frowning.

He got up and grabbed a flashlight. He passed the beam of light around the room, but saw nothing.

Outside his door, the sound of a dog's footsteps caused Butch to jump. He slowly crept toward the door. He opened the door quickly and shined the flashlight into the hallway. He turned on the hallway light and looked at the floor. Muddy paw prints led away from his door and down the hall to the living room. He inched forward slowly, nervously rubbed his face and scratched his head.

Butch flipped the light on in the living room as he entered. The trail of paw prints led him to the closet next to the front door. Butch slowly opened the closet door and jumped.

A wet, broken leather leash lay on the floor of the closet.

Butch stumbled back. *Didn't I...?* he thought.

His mind flashed back to when he swung the dog on the end of the leash to get momentum and the leash broke, releasing the dog into the swollen rushing waters.

Butch turned and ran into the kitchen. He opened drawers frantically, searching through the contents.

"Gloves, gloves, gloves... dammit!"

Butch slammed the drawers shut. He looked over at the dish drainer and spotted a pair of tongs. He grabbed the tongs, went back into the living room and picked up the leash with the tongs. He opened his back door and peered around cautiously to make sure no one was watching him.

Butch walked across the field toward the bayou, holding the leash using the tongs so he didn't touch it. He reached the water, looked around again to be sure he wasn't being watched, and then tossed the leash into the water.

"Dead dogs tell no tales," he sneered.

When Butch got back into the house, he frantically mopped up the muddy paw prints. He inspected his cleanup job thoroughly to insure there was no trace of mud in the house. He turned off the light and returned to a not very restful night of sleep.

The next day, the two officers knocked on the front door. Butch wandered out into the living room, looking like he just woke up, and answered the door.

"Officers?"

"Sorry to disturb you so early, Mister Sellers. May we come in?"

"Sure," Butch replied and let them in. The officers walked to the center of the living room. The officer who did the questioning the night before pointed to the pictures on the walls. Butch looked at where he pointed and rubbed the sleep out of his eyes.

"We noticed there are a lot of pictures of the dog."

"Yeah," Butch said as he yawned. "Like I said, she really loved that dog."

"There are no pictures of you."

"I'm not very photogenic," Butch said and shrugged his shoulders.

"Mister Sellers, we noticed you have a one hundred thousand dollar life insurance policy on your wife."

"And a five hundred thousand dollar policy on myself. That's really pretty standard for a family isn't it?"

The officer nodded.

"You don't seem to have any major financial obligations. Your house and car are paid for. You really have no outstanding debts. Why so much money for your wife's death?"

"Guys, it's just precautionary. My insurance agent recommended that amount to cover funeral and miscellaneous expenses. I just followed his recommendation. You want to give him a call?"

"Were you two happily married?"

"You already asked that question."

"You said how long you had been married; you didn't actually answer the question."

"Well, we definitely had our disagreements," Butch said as he shrugged his shoulders. His mind recalled a particularly loud disagreement.

"You love that dog more than me!" he shouted at Melinda, standing in the same living room. Tears streamed down her face.

"Butch," she said, her voice quivering.

"I come home to have steak and you've fed it to that mutt? The dog chews up my shoes and you stand up for it? Hell, Melinda, you let it pee on my side of the bed!"

Melinda's temper rose as Butch spoke. Her anger replaced her fear.

"Well, at least it knows how to show affection!"

"That's it, the dog's going." Butch folded his arms and stared daggers at Melinda. She stared them right back.

"Over my dead body!"

Butch smirked at the officers.

"But we never had any serious arguments. I'm going to grab a cup of coffee. It was a long night."

Butch walked into the kitchen, followed by the officers. He walked over to the counter and turned on the coffee maker.

"One of Melinda's close friends said you two argued about the dog quite a bit."

"I do recall raising my voice about the dog not being properly housebroken. Maybe that got blown out of proportion. I mean, we don't have any children. The dog was family. I think she spoiled him a little, but what was I going to say about that?"

"We're just tracking down leads, Mister Sellers."

"Look, my life's an open book. I just wish you could find her, so we could put this all to rest."

"You don't think your wife is dead?"

"I don't know. If you find her dead or alive, we can put this to rest. I can't sleep well wondering what happened to her."

"You plan on leaving town any time soon, Mister Sellers?"

In his mind, Butch lounged on a beach chair in Acapulco, the cool sea breeze ruffling his straw hat.

"No. Why?"

"Don't make any plans. I'm sure we'll be back to ask a few more questions."

"Can I ask you a question?"

"Sure."

"While you're here badgering me about something I may or may not have done to my wife, you do have people looking for her still, right? You haven't given up on her, have you?"

"We have teams looking for her now."

Butch spotted the muddy tongs he left on the counter last night.

"Good. Anything else I can answer for you?" Butch maneuvered in front of the tongs. He opened a cabinet door and took out a coffee cup.

"No, Mister Sellers. I apologize if this was painful. We're just doing our jobs."

"Yeah, I know."

"Thank you for your time. We'll be seeing you again soon."

"I'm sure. I'll see you out," Butch said as he gestured toward the living room and the officers walked that way. Butch set the coffee cup on the counter in front of the muddy end of the tongs and followed the officers out. He saw them to the door and watched through the window as they walked to their car. He turned around and started to walk back to the kitchen, but stopped suddenly. In front of the fireplace, in plain sight, laid the broken piece of leash on top of a pair of gloves identical to the ones he used the night of the killings.

Butch's eye twitched.

After glancing out the window, Butch put a few logs into the fireplace and quickly lit them. He calmly walked to the kitchen, poured a cup of coffee and walked back into the living room. The temperature outside was in the seventies. No need for a fire really, but Butch was definitely chilled to the bone as he looked at the roaring fire and tossed the leash and gloves into the flames. He pulled a chair in front of the fireplace, grabbed his coffee from an end table and sat down to watch the items burn in the fireplace.

"Gonna stay gone this time, aren't ya. I'm watching you."

That night, Butch again slept fitfully, tossing and turning in bed.

Melinda stood next to Butch's bed, covered in weeds and mud, holding the leash and gloves in her hands.

"Did you lose these?"

Butch jerked awake. He blinked into the darkness. He could feel the dark circles under his eyes from lack of sleep. He lay down again and closed his eyes.

"She's dead… she's dead… she's dead…" he whispered over and over until he fell asleep again.

The next day, Butch walked out onto his sunlit porch, breathing in the warm air. He rested his hand on a windowsill and bent down to pick up the newspaper. A cold wet hand reached through the open window and grabbed his arm. Butch jumped and shouted in surprise. The hand disappeared quickly and Butch peered into the darkness trying to see what was in the house.

"You heard anything?" a voice said from behind him. Butch

jumped a little and turned around to see David, his brother-in-law, walking up to the porch. Butch regained his composure quickly.

"No. They haven't found any sign of Melinda or Fifi."

"I still can't believe she's gone," David said. He swallowed away the pain. "It's been a week. You think she might still be alive?"

"We can only pray, David. It's in God's hands now."

"Yeah. Well, I was just stopping by to see how you're holding up."

Butch glanced in the door and saw wet footprints on the floor. He quickly looked back at David. "As well as can be expected. Just taking it day by day. I'm starting to lose hope though. It's tough."

"Hey, just keep praying. That's all we can do. We all just want to see her again, don't we? Give me a call if you need anything, okay?"

"You betcha. Thanks."

"No problem. Take care."

David turned and left. Butch watched him leave. He looked back into the house, then back at David. His hands fidgeted nervously as he watched David climb into his car and drive away. Butch remained on the porch and watched David's car until in disappeared from view completely, glancing periodically into the house. When David was finally out of sight, Butch turned back to the house and quickly opened the door.

Butch walked in and looked at the wet footprints on the floor. He avoided them and walked over to the fireplace. He retrieved the poker and held it at the ready as he carefully looked around the living room, behind furniture, searching for the source of the mysterious prints. He briefly poked his head into the kitchen, but didn't see anything there and returned to the living room.

He followed the trail of wet footprints to the bathroom door. He held the poker at the ready to strike and quickly opened the door with his other hand.

Wet footprints on the linoleum floor led to the bathtub, hidden behind a shower curtain. Butch slowly approached the curtain, nervously watching it for any signs of movement.

He held the poker at the ready again and pulled the curtain aside. There was nothing in the bathtub. Butch lowered the poker and chuckled.

"Crazy…"

Butch turned to leave and was met by his dead wife staring at him, covered in mud and weeds. Butch panicked and quickly raised the poker. He lost his footing on the wet linoleum floor and grabbed wildly for something to steady him. His hand fell on the shower curtain, which he pulled loose as Butch fell face first onto the bathroom floor; the poker in his other hand pierced his throat, ripping open his jugular vein.

Butch struggled to sit up. He managed to get into a sitting position, grabbed his throat with one hand, and pushed himself up with the other hand on the toilet. Blood gushed out from under his hand down the front of his shirt. He came to rest against the wall next to the toilet.

Melinda stared silently into his face and then faded from view. Butch died with his eyes open, his blood streamed onto the floor, mixing with the gentle trickle of water coming from a small leak from under the bathroom sink.

When the police found him, they determined his death had been a terrible accident. No one could figure out why Butch had a fireplace poker in the bathroom, though.

THE VISION

Well, that's it then," Helena said and let go of Frank's hand.

"I don't believe it," Frank replied as he absently rubbed his hand where Helena had traced his life line. It had come up short.

"It's not my first time, ya know."

"Really, how many other deaths have you predicted?" Frank rolled his eyes.

"You predicted it. I just interpreted your vision and confirmed it with your lifeline. Incredibly short and you know you're hit by a city bus in two weeks. Dead. End of story. So, you should get all your affairs in order and say your goodbyes."

"I'm just supposed to take your word for it?"

"I said this wasn't my first time. Check with Bill Dominick's family on 6th and Gilcrest. He'll die tomorrow from a lightning strike."

"There's no rain tomorrow."

"Don't need rain for lightning."

"Fine. I'll pay a visit to Bill and pay my respects to him personally."

Frank got up and walked away.

"What, no tip?" Helena shouted.

"I'll give you a tip in three weeks!" Frank shouted and then opened the door and walked out into the chilled night air.

"Cheap dead bastard!" he heard Helena shout after him. He shook his head and continued walking. He was sure she was a crackpot.

Frank was so sure Helena was crazy that he totally forgot to go see Bill the next day. It wasn't until the following day, when he saw a news story about a man dying from a freak lightning strike while playing golf that Frank thought there might be something to it.

"Bill said he didn't want to die at work," his widow said. "So after he put his affairs in order, he set a tee time on the golf course for the day he said he was going to die. We never thought it would happen. But I did have him scheduled for a psych appointment this morning. I'm just sorry he couldn't make the appointment."

Bill's widow cried and nothing more could be gotten from her. Frank turned the television off. He got up, grabbed his coat and walked out the door.

Fifteen minutes later, he was at Helena's door. The 'OPEN' light was dark and so was most of the house. It was only after waking up all the neighborhood dogs from his incessant pounding on Helena's door that she showed up and let him in.

"Closed for the night, can't you read?"

"How do I stop it?" Frank demanded.

"Stop what?" Helena asked. "Wait, you have to pay ahead of time for a reading, so before you start asking questions..."

"Bill's dead. Lightning strike."

"Yeah? And?"

"He knew it was coming, but he obviously didn't try to stop it or did he? What did you tell him to do?"

"Get his affairs in order. Hopefully he did. I didn't follow-up with him since I knew he wasn't going to be a repeat customer."

"How do I stop it?"

"How should I know? Prayer?"

"You have to know something you aren't telling."

"Frank, get your affairs in order, say goodbye to your loved ones, donate time and money to charity. What else are you going to do with the time you have left?"

"Fight it."

"Tell you what. How about if I give you a refund and we forget this ever happened?"

"Sounds great."

"Fine. I'll give you a refund in three weeks."

"Very funny."

"You can't fight fate, Frank."

Frank opened the door. "Watch me," he said and walked out.

"Only if you were going to be a repeat customer," Helena said and shut the door.

Dead Day Minus Twelve

Frank awoke feeling refreshed. He called in sick to work. *No use in wasting vacation days,* he mused. Ironically, the last person he'd want to benefit from his unused vacation days would be Darla, his ex-wife. If he beat fate, he'd take a nice vacation. If he didn't, his pension and unused vacation would go to Darla and the kids. But, he intended to beat fate with a bloody vengeance.

Forty-five minutes later, Frank was walking around the docks when he saw the man he was looking for. Dan Britano and Frank had been buddies growing up. They'd been the best of friends until the mob came calling. Frank went into the military to get away from it. Dan embraced the life and the lifestyle. No telling how many bodies had been buried at Dan's order. Ironically, he may have exceeded his friend's death count while he was in the military, carrying out orders. Perhaps there was no escaping his role in life as an executioner. He waved at his old, deadly friend.

"Frank! You old son of a gun!" Dan said and ran over to Frank. His two associates kept a watchful distance. Out of earshot, but not out of range for the concealed weapons they carried.

"Dan, still playing on the docks, I see," Frank said.

"Like you could drag me away!" Dan shook his hand warmly. "My God, it's been a couple years, hasn't it? How old is Jeannie now?"

"She's nine and every bit as stubborn as her mother."

"Darla," Dan smiled and nodded. "She's a firecracker, all right. Then you got two boys, right?"

"Frankie junior and Ricky."

"Nice. Sorry it all got broke up, though."

"That PTSD demon rears its ugly head too many times to stay in a relationship."

Dan looked out over the water and nodded his head. "I love reminiscing, Frank. But I'm pretty sure that wasn't why you looked me up today. Something you don't want to discuss over the phone?"

"I need a favor, Dan. It's kinda big."

"Hey, we're brothers from way back. You need a loan? I can get whatever you need."

"I need the bus drivers to go on strike in twelve days. No buses on the road at all."

Dan looked out over the water again and scratched his chin. He shrugged his shoulders. "I don't have that kind of pull, Frank."

"You have the teamsters in your back pocket, Dan."

"That was four years ago, Frank. There've been some changes in the organization."

"Can you call in a favor?"

"If I had like six months notice, I could probably arrange a few things, make some things happen, but twelve days…"

"It's a matter of life and death, Dan."

"Okay, lemme think." Dan looked out over the water again. His mouth moved silently and he fidgeted with his hands. Frank recognized the mannerisms from all the way back in childhood. When Dan had to work on something complex, his mouth would move along with his thoughts and his hands fidgeted, moving options around in his mind. Dan clasped his hands together.

"Going to have to think outside the box on this one, Frank. Although, it's really more in your box."

Frank took a deep breath. "Who?"

"Are sure this is life or death? This is huge," Dan said.

"My life, Dan. I'm sure. I can't leave those kids without a dad."

Dan took a deep breath in and blew it out. "There are three guys in line before me stepping into that position. If you can take them out in the next five days, that will give me enough time to push a strike through."

"Thanks, Dan."

"I get a promotion, you save your life. Sounds like a reasonable trade."

"Who are they?"

"Alfonso Milanni—he's got the position now. You can find him in the financial sector. He likes to rub elbows with bankers. Thinks he's going to move up in the organization soon. Believe it or not, he's going to be easier than the next guy. Vincent Vicelli is one paranoid son of a bitch. He's probably going to be your toughest hit. He likes to hang out with his judge buddies at the courthouse—mostly because it's so hard to get a weapon into there that he feels safe during the day."

"Last but not least is Jimmy Toonis. You can find him stocking shelves at Drago's Market."

"Stocking shelves?"

"It's a front. He's laying low while some heat passes on him."

"All right." Frank took a deep breath and smiled grimly. "See you in a couple of days."

Dead Day Minus Eleven

Alfonso wasn't much of a challenge initially. Frank followed him into an elevator alone, cold cocked him and waited for the elevator to get to the under construction tenth floor. Then Frank sent him on a tumble down the stairs, breaking his neck on the way down when his head got caught in the railing. A little grisly to watch, but Frank had seen so much worse in theater that it barely phased him; that was until he heard the sickening crack of Alfonso's skull on the cement slab of the stair landing.

The sandy killing fields came rushing back into Frank's mind, highlighted by the sickening crack and smell of a days old dead body bursting open under pressure from its own decomposing gases. Frank was at the rear of the squad when the body performed its popping show for him. The smell and sight drove him to the edge of a broken wall where he heaved his guts out. He wasn't in the death zone when the rain of bullets took out the rest of his squad. Frank scrambled behind the wall for cover.

From behind the rubble, Frank watched the villainous vipers emerge from the shadows carrying their own weapons scavenged from dead men. He watched them move among the dead and almost dead. One of them fired another shot into a groaning squad member.

The moaning ceased. Frank vaguely remembers a red haze passing over his vision and a symphony of gun fire erupting from his weapon, mowing down the enemy that thought they had killed or mortally injured his entire squad. It wasn't until nothing else moved or lived of the enemy that Frank's gun went silent. Two of his squad still lived, though they were injured so badly they'd never see action again. Frank called in a med evac and was sighing a breath of relief when his eyes lingered on one of the dead bodies amongst the enemy. It was a child, maybe twelve years old. The child's body was riddled with bullets from his gun.

That was the injury to Frank's mind that ensured he'd never see action in theater again. He got a medal for saving his two squad members, but he never passed the psych evaluation to go back.

Frank opened his eyes and looked at the ceiling of the stairwell. He sat up and realized he was soaking wet from sweat. He didn't know how long he'd been out. He stumbled up to the next floor and made his way quietly to the elevator, never seeing a soul on the next floor as it was nearly completely unoccupied. He rode down the elevator and, like a zombie on remote control, made his way out the door amongst the small crowd that had gathered in the elevator on its descent.

Dead Day Minus Ten

Frank tried but couldn't bring himself to move out of bed all day. He gave in and took some of the meds he'd received for anxiety. They knocked him out most of the day.

Every time he opened his eyes, a curious, dead twelve year-old boy stared back at him, face gaunt with blood loss, dirt and hunger. Frank spent much of the day with his head under the covers.

Dead Day Minus Nine

There was no escaping the ticking clock of fate. Frank dragged himself from his bed and avoided looking at the mirror until he'd made it through the shower. It was a fruitless delay. After his shower, one glance in the mirror told him if fate didn't kill him, his fight against it might. The deep circles under his eyes showed that his rest the entire day before had been for naught. Not that he'd opt for another day of bed rest; it just wasn't as therapeutic as he'd hoped.

Anticipating a tougher kill, Frank pulled out his old sniper rifle and cleaned it. He took it completely apart and put it back together, several times. He did it a few more times with his eyes closed. The ritual was calming and therapeutic—more so than the sleep had been.

Dan's warning about Vincent Vicelli turned out to be more than accurate. Vincent was cagier than Alfonso by a factor of a thousand. He had a security team three times the size of the president. Frank shadowed him all day, but could never get close enough to do anything. Even a well placed sniper shot was nigh impossible. Vincent kept to cars and building interiors, staying away from windows whenever possible. He was paranoid to the nth degree.

When Vincent went home for the day, Frank saw his opportunity. The entire house was surrounded by floodlights, keeping it illuminated during the night to prevent intruders from gaining access. That also lit up the exterior gas line to the house—Frank's new target. One hit from the rifle and the house would go up.

Frank scouted out the homes across from the rear of Vincent's place. He found a vacant mansion for sale, noted the address and drove out of the neighborhood to the nearby golf course parking lot. There was a large event at the facility and the parking lot was well populated. Frank changed into jogging gear and put a light backpack on that resembled a water pouch. It actually contained his broken down sniper rifle, silencer and ammunition.

As he jogged into the neighborhood, Frank was actually difficult to spot. The jogging clothes were dark and he wore no reflective clothing. Anyone who didn't know better would just think he was a foolish jogger. When he got to the house he noted earlier, Frank double-checked to be sure no one was watching and then slipped into the backyard. The house was dark. Frank jimmied the lock on the back door and gained entrance. There was no alarm since there was nothing in the house and no electricity.

Frank used the light from his phone to navigate to the upstairs and to a window facing Vincent's house. He setup the rifle in the dark as he'd been trained to do hundreds of times. He opened the window, removed the screen and set the rifle barrel on the windowsill to line up the shot. As he looked through the scope, he saw Vincent's living room with Vincent, his wife and their two children. The children were in pajamas and headed for bed.

Frank took the rifle down from the windowsill and sat with his back against the wall. His hand started to shake. He set the rifle down and just let the shake take over his whole body. There had to be some sort of penance for killing the whole family. He would slaughter innocent children he hoped would be killed instantly and not burn to death screaming in agony. The sweat broke out on his forehead and the tears streamed down his face.

Frank wasn't sure how much time had passed when it occurred to him he could just kill Vincent from afar. Sure, he might get caught. They'd trace the bullet back to here and maybe pick up some DNA leading to him. Chance he'd have to take to not kill the kids.

He set the rifle back in the window and looked down the scope at a completely dark interior. He'd taken too long. They'd all gone to bed and everything was pitch black inside. Frank swiveled quickly and found the gas terminal and let the bullet fly that lit the house up. The explosion shattered the windows above his head and set off car alarms for blocks away in all directions.

Frank sat for a while watching the geyser of flame shoot up in the air. The shattered remains of Vincent's house, the occupants and even the guards laid strewn out about a hundred feet from the center of the explosion. Frank took his gun apart without looking at it. He glanced down to place the pieces back in the backpack. He took one last look at his handiwork and then walked out of the room with his backpack slung onto his back. He didn't bother closing the back door as he walked out. It would appear to be blown open as all the windows had been blown out. Frank walked numbly from the backyard and out onto the street. Panicked neighbors were climbing in their cars and driving from the neighborhood into the dark night. No one noticed the pedestrian jogger walking by.

Dead Day Minus Eight

Man falls down a stairwell and it's an accident. Not even reported in the news. The gas line rupture would take a lot of investigation. Frank wondered if they'd ever find what was left of the armor piercing round he used.

Fate drove him to this, he decided. The deaths could rest on fate's shoulders, not his.

"It's not my fault," Frank said to the twelve year old dead boy staring at him from across the room, flanked by the two younger dead children with seared flesh hanging from the exposed skeletal framework of their bodies.

"Fate shouldn't mess with me," Frank said as the drugs pushed him into a fitful unconsciousness. Throughout the day, his eyes fluttered open and he saw the dead children staring at him silently. They never said anything, but their accusing glares were worth a thousand judgmental words.

Dead Day Minus Seven

Frank left the sniper rifle at home. When he tracked down Jimmy Toonis, he would vent his rage against fate on the unfortunate target. Frank had arrayed upon his person a bevy of up-close and personal execution tools. The razor wire was the most effective and had the added benefit of rendering the victim silent when applied correctly.

When Frank arrived at the grocery, it took a bit of shopping before he met his target. In the open aisle and bright lights of the store, it was easy to see young Jimmy had barely graduated from high school. The fresh faced and friendly stocker was hardly the target Frank was expecting. This was the type of kid he wished his daughter would find when she reached dating age. He was no mobster. Even so, this was his final target. No reason to back down now, just one killing away from defeating fate.

During a casual discussion in one of the aisles, Jimmy mentioned the only part of the job he hated was taking out the garbage at the end of the day. Frank agreed that sounded particularly horrible. They said their goodbyes. Frank left the building and made his way around to the dumpsters, scoping out the best area to lay the ambush.

As he lay in wait for Jimmy to finish his job, Frank got three visitors. The three dead children eyed him scornfully and crossed their arms. This was a particularly grisly affair for the children with the tattered remains of burned flesh hanging from their bones. Frank tried to not look at them, but their very presence compelled him to meet their gaze. When Jimmy came out of the grocery store dragging two large garbage bags behind him, Frank tightened his grip on the razor wire, but ultimately couldn't bring himself to leap from the darkness and strangle Jimmy. Instead, he sat in the darkness as the bags made their cushioned clang inside the metal box and he listened to Jimmy's footsteps fade away.

Dead Day Minus Six

"Dan, this one's just a kid," Frank said as he walked along the dock with his friend.

"Look, he's already done time in juvie for running drugs for his pop's organization, so don't tell me this kid's innocent. I know him and his family." Dan flicked his cigarette off the pier. Several seagulls dived for it. The victor seemed happy to fly away into the early morning sun with his prize.

"He's barely old enough to tie his own shoes, for chrissake," Frank replied. He stopped and looked out over the water. Dan stopped and put his arm around him.

"You remember how old we were when we hit our first convenience store? How about our first shakedown, huh? We were barely outta diapers."

Frank nodded but didn't seem convinced.

"Look, Frank, it's no skin off my back. You don't want to finish the trifecta, that's fine. I just can't help you with your problem while he's still alive. Once the organization figures out the other two are dead, it's just a matter of maybe a day or two before this kid gets put into place. He may be unreachable by then even by you. Help me help you."

Frank sniffed the morning air and nodded. "You're right, Dan. I just gotta pull myself together and get it over with," Frank turned to his friend and smiled. "You're doing right by me. It's the least I can do."

Donning a disguise and gloves to keep the DNA traces down, Frank stole a car a few hours later and waited in the parking lot of the grocery store for Jimmy to arrive at work. As he sat in the car waiting, he glanced in the rear view mirror and saw the children staring at him from the back seat.

"Stop giving me the guilt trip—this kid's dirty and you know it," Frank said to the juvenile ghosts. As was typical, they didn't respond verbally but simply continued to stare at him, darts of accusations flew into the back of his head with every passing moment.

Finally, Jimmy arrived in his beat-up car and parked at the far side of the parking lot. Frank crept closer until Jimmy glanced his direction. Seeing the car not moving, Jimmy figured the driver was letting him cross the aisle to go to work. Just before Jimmy reached the halfway mark, Frank slammed his foot down on the accelerator and the car lurched forward. Jimmy had only a few seconds to try to dodge the oncoming car and nearly managed it, but got crushed between the stolen vehicle and a parked car. Jimmy's anguished face was the last thing Frank saw of the teenager before leaving the parking lot burning rubber.

After abandoning the car, Frank walked the ten blocks to his own vehicle. As he walked, he would pass windows filled with the three kids now joined by Jimmy staring out at him. The four specters haunted his every move now. Frank considered going straight home to a bottle of pills, but shook his head to clear his mind. He had to see Dan and get the mobster working on his problem now that he was free to act.

As night fell, Frank drove to his friend's neighborhood and parked a few blocks away. When the sunlight had completely disappeared, Frank made his way to Dan's home. Avoiding the guards there, Frank got up the stairs and into the study where Dan usually spent his evenings after dinner looking at his books. Frank crept into the room and Dan didn't notice him until the door clicked shut. Startled, Dan whirled around.

"Frank! Jeez, you nearly gave me a heart attack," Dan said.

"It's done. Now you fulfill your part of the bargain," Frank said as he slid his hands into his jacket pockets.

"Yeah," Dan said. "About that. I'm afraid I cannot honor your request. It would take too much money out of my pocket."

"What? I just killed three people so you could get in this position to help me!"

"No you didn't," Dan said. "I was in the position all along."

"Then why did you want these guys dead?"

"Oh, well, Alfonso, he insulted me once. Took my spot at the table for a very special dinner." Dan sat down and lit a cigar. "Now Victor, he disrespected me. Took a kid out of my neighborhood and brought him into his own organization. Didn't ask me squat. Just took the kid. Very uncool."

"What about Jimmy?"

"Yeah, Jimmy. He was dating my daughter. I thought he was a little too clean for our family. She's very distraught about it, of course. But, accidents happen." Dan took a big puff of his cigar and smiled.

"Accidents happen," Frank said and walked menacingly toward Dan.

"Ah ah!" Dan said and clicked a remote. A video started playing on the screen. It showed Frank sitting in the stolen car before he hit Jimmy.

"Now, you surprised me with Alfonso. I thought we'd be able to watch wherever you went, but you picked a building we didn't have under surveillance. Victor, well, I never thought you'd torch his whole family. A bit unpredictable but very thorough there. Jimmy—we had you in a clear video the night you were gonna garrote him, but then you chickened out."

Frank pulled out a knife.

"Anything happens to me, Frank, and this footage goes to the cops via a route I ain't going to tell you about."

"You stupid fuck," Frank said. "You're not stopping the buses, which means I die in five days. Why the fuck should I care about a goddamn video sent to the cops?!"

Dan's mouth formed a smug grin and his brow wrinkled.

"Hey, you know what? You want those buses stopped, I'll do it. No problem."

"You lying sack of shit," Frank said and threw the knife. It sunk into Dan's forehead, knocking him back into the seat. His head slumped forward.

Dead Day Minus Five

Frank sat in front of the television watching the news on a hit and run driver that killed Jimmy. Police were asking for leads as they'd come to a dead end. Frank took another swig from the bottle of whiskey in his hand.

On the sofa across the room, his four victims watched silently. The stares made Frank sneer and take another drink.

Dead Day Minus Four

Frank walked into the cathedral. He glanced at the schedule to double check it was time for confession. The pews were filling up with the early birds, but this was also when pre-Mass confession took place.

Frank entered the familiar door and took a seat in the tiny booth, closing the door behind him.

After a time, the small door between the booths opens.

"Good evening, my son."

Frank made the sign of the cross and then sighed. "Forgive me Father, for I have sinned. It's been, uh, about twelve years since my last confession. I've, well, I've hurt a lot of people, Father."

"Hurt?"

Frank looked down and took a deep breath.

"I hurt my wife and kids with my outbursts. It all came from the killings while I was in the military."

"I see."

"Father, there were a lot of deaths at my hand in the military."

"I know your country thanks you for your service. But, you are right to mourn the deaths of those you've killed."

"And I've been active more recently, Father."

"Active?"

"I'm going to be dying in a few days. I thought I could prevent it, but I tried to get help from some people who asked me to do terrible things."

Tears came to Frank's eyes. "I just didn't want to leave my kids without a father, you know. But it was all for nothing. I'm still dying and there's nothing anyone can do about it."

"You shouldn't be killing people."

"I know. It was... a momentary lapse in judgment. I won't do it again for the rest of my life."

Frank laughs. "All four days of it."

"I can give you penance, son, to save your soul, but you should be talking to the police and telling them what you've done. It's the only way you'll be free of the guilt."

"Okay, Father. I'll think about that."

Frank finished his confessional and left the small booth. He walked in front of the Jesus statue and made the sign of the cross. He lingered for a moment and stared at the marble statue hanging there.

"See you soon," he whispered and walked out.

Dead Day Minus Three

Frank stared at the ceiling as the sunlight crept across it. He wasn't sure how long he laid there after waking. It had been a fitful night of fractured sleep. The phone rang. Frank jumped up and ran into the kitchen. He looked at the calendar, which he had blacked out three days from now—a not so subtle reminder that fate's deadline was approaching.

More important than fate's deadline, however, was this particular Saturday. This was his visitation with the kids. He grabbed the phone.

"Hello?"

"Are you coming today, Frank? I can do other things if you're going to blow it off again." Darla, his cantankerous ex-wife, put the grating in her voice that had driven him away.

He took a deep breath. "Sorry, I'm on my way."

Frank hung up the phone before she could reply. He knew she hated that. It was his one thing he could do to needle her without getting the authorities in a bind. Not that it would matter in a few days, he reasoned.

He quickly changed clothes and dabbed some deodorant on to make himself somewhat decent to smell. He realized he hadn't taken a shower in a few days. The stress of killing so many in such a short time was taking its toll. He felt like he wasn't likely done. He opened his medication and dumped a pill onto the counter. He closed the bottle and brought it down on the pill, splitting it into several pieces. He put together what looked like about one fourth of a pill and swallowed it down with some water.

On the way to Darla's house, he stopped in for a quick adjustment with his insurance agent. After a quick discussion, he bumped up his life insurance $500,000—most he could do without a health checkup. When Frank mentioned he wanted to pay the premium now since he was going to be traveling and didn't want to miss it, the agent tacked on an extra $250,000 travel insurance rider just in case he had an accident when he went abroad. Frank thanked him for thinking of it as travel was much more dangerous nowadays.

He stopped and grabbed a dozen roses for Darla. It had been years since he'd given her flowers. His mind wandered briefly to the good times before they'd grown apart. He shook his head and focused on driving. Fate could injure him before it decided to kill him in three days.

When he entered the house, the kids ran to him and hugged him. It was the kind of unconditional love children gave people when they didn't know any better. His angels had no idea he was a killer. They just knew him as Daddy.

He handed the roses to Jeannie.

"Tell your mom these are from her three wonderful children," Frank said. Jeannie beamed a smile at him. The children ran out of the room with the flowers. Frank often brought flowers home and presented them the same way back when they were still a family. Last time had been about three years ago, before Frank's illness and stubbornness to not take the medication had finally split them apart.

The kids returned and hugged him again. Eventually, Darla appeared in the hall and looked at him with a tilt of her head.

"Can we go to the kids' museum?" Frank asked.

"Frank, you know you can't be unsupervised," Darla said.

'I mean all of us, like a big happy family."

"Frank, I can't afford—"

"My treat. I'm on my meds, I'll be a perfect gentleman," Frank said and smiled.

"Please, Mom?" Jeannie said as she tugged on Darla's arm. Darla sighed.

"I suppose. Just let me get changed. Boys, put your shoes on."

For a day, Frank got to pretend to be a full-time father and husband again. Seeing his children scamper along the hallways and exhibits having a blast was priceless. He even enjoyed Darla's company after refusing to fight with her for the first two hours after which she gave up trying and just enjoyed the day along with him. It was the best day of the last three years.

Dead Day Minus Two

On the flight to the U.S. Virgin Islands, Frank rested semi-comfortably. The coach seats left little room for brooding ghosts. They only visited him when he shut his eyes for more than five minutes. Luckily, the flight wasn't too long and he only had to be told to keep it down three times.

Dead Day Minus One

Frank awoke to a gorgeous sunrise. He drank piña coladas by the shore and danced the night away. He lay on the bed in his hotel room, gave the finger to the ghosts waiting there for him and passed out.

Dead Day

A fire alarm awoke Frank from his stupor. He stumbled out of the hotel into the street with the other hotel guests. He smiled as he realized he hadn't been killed by a city bus. Then a recycled city bus blew a tire and its brakes went out as it plowed sideways through the group of hotel guests. It fell over, pinning Frank to the ground, crushing his legs and pelvis. As he lay there bleeding out, the four ghosts gave him the finger and he died.

Planting Seeds of the Future

Sheriff Tom Miller sat down at the counter in Wanda's Waffles. Wanda brought him his customary pile of waffles and raspberry syrup, butter on the side. He picked up his fork and poked at the butter. Wanda watched him for a moment as she filled his coffee.

"You usually start devouring those as soon as they hit the linoleum," Wanda said as she walked away with the coffee pot and put it back on the burner.

"Yup," Tom said and continued to poke the butter calmly.

"Ya done everything ya can for them kids, Tom," she said as she brought him a glass of milk. "Even called in the FBI. I'm pretty sure ya didn't call the press, though."

Outside the restaurant, there were dozens of news vans as far as the eye could see. Main street wasn't that big, but it was crowded.

"Two went missing two nights ago. That's after the FBI showed up," Tom said and took a swig of coffee. "Not sure they're much help. They got a male in his mid thirties pegged for the abductor. That really narrows it down to most of southern Illinois."

"They'll turn up, Tom. No one can hide something this big

for long."

Old Leroy Watkins walked in just then and sat down next to Tom. Wanda nodded at him, wrote something on a tab of paper and handed it back to the short order cook.

"Gee doggy, there sure are a lot of visitors this morning!" Leroy exclaimed. Wanda poured him a cup of coffee and he drank it hot and black right then.

"What brings you into town, Leroy?" Tom said and started spreading his butter on the waffles.

"The future, Tom! Ain't that what all them folks out there are here for?"

"Well," Tom said. "It's not the kind of future I had envisioned."

"Not too much we can control about the future anymore, Tom. That's the problem with life nowadays." Leroy finished his coffee and held it up for Wanda. She walked back to get the coffee pot.

"The future's here, gentlemen," Wanda said. "It's always been coming. Television, cell phones, internet. Everything's connected."

"Think I'd like it to come a little slower then." Tom smirked.

"Say, Tom," Leroy said as he smiled at Wanda refilling his cup. There was a ding and Wanda went to go pickup Leroy's food. "Why are the schools closed?"

Tom was just putting a piece of waffle in his mouth, but stopped short when Leroy asked the question.

"You don't have school age kids, Leroy."

"Nope," Leroy said as he cut into the over easy eggs. "But how we gonna get to the future without kids attending school?"

"Mmm," Tom said and started eating his food again. He shook his head.

Getting too damn suspicious in my old age, he thought.

Tom finished his food and pushed it aside while he washed it down with a little more coffee. Leroy had just finished as well and was working on what Tom figured was his fourth cup of coffee.

"Had enough coffee yet, Leroy?" Tom said with a small chuckle.

Leroy looked at him strange. "Just had two cups. Isn't that how many you had?"

Wanda refilled Leroy's cup again.

"That's your fifth cup, Leroy," Wanda said and returned the carafe to the machine to make a new batch.

Leroy looked confused. "Well, I guess I just lost track," he said. He put the cup down and scratched his stubble. "Maybe I'm not as sharp as I used to be."

"Think we can all say that, Leroy," Tom replied.

"That might explain my problem," Leroy said as he nodded. "Say, Tom, you used to be a farmer way back when, right?"

"I grew up on my Daddy's farm, Leroy. See, you remember all sorts of things."

"I'm having a problem germinating this latest crop. I've tried everything, but I can't get a sprout to pop up. Think you can stop by and take a look?"

"Sure thing, Leroy. Might be just the break I need to clear my head."

Leroy put a few bills on the counter and stood up. "See you later, then," he said and walked out.

Tom watched him go. When Leroy was out of sight, Tom turned to Wanda. "Leroy been forgetting things a lot?"

"I just thought he really liked his coffee," Wanda said and shrugged. "He's been drinking a lot more of it the last couple months."

"Damn shame," Tom said. He put a few bills on the counter and walked out the door.

Tom pulled up outside Leroy's farm with his deputy Walter riding shotgun. They needed to make an assessment to see if Leroy might need to be taken into custody to protect him from himself. They got out of the car and approached the farmhouse when Leroy suddenly appeared on the porch with a shotgun. He brandished it at the men, who immediately ducked down behind the police car to take cover.

"What are ya'll doing on my property?!" Leroy shouted.

"Leroy," Tom shouted back. "It's Tom, remember from breakfast? You asked me to stop by and look at your new crop. You said it wasn't sprouting."

"Oh yeah, come on up," Leroy replied. The two officers looked over the top of the car and saw Leroy set the shotgun down on the porch and go into the house.

"Okay, Walter," Tom whispered. "Why don't you radio for some backup just in case we have any more firearms to deal with?"

Walter nodded and sat back down in their cruiser. Tom stood up and walked to the porch.

"Hey, Leroy. This is Tom; I'm coming in, all right?"

"Sure," Leroy replied from inside the house. "Come on in!"

Tom opened the door slowly and was assaulted by the strong smell of fertilizer coming from the house. He saw Leroy measuring an amount from one bag and putting it in a bucket. Then he took some from another bag and measured it out. There were seven different bags in the living room spread out. Tom looked at the walls and saw educational and inspirational posters stapled to them. The messages were "Children are the Hope of Tomorrow," "Children are the Future," and "Plant the Seeds of Knowledge Today for a Brighter Future."

"Oh hell," Tom whispered. Leroy seemed oblivious to Tom's presence as he continued to scoop and measure different amounts of fertilizer.

"Leroy, where's this new crop you want me to take a look at?" Tom had his hand on his gun just in case. Leroy turned around and seemed surprised to see Tom.

"Oh, yeah, the new crop! Right this way," Leroy brightened up and walked out the back door, dropping the fertilizer he was measuring on the floor. Judging from the mess on the floor, he'd done this many times already. Tom followed Leroy through the kitchen and out the back door.

As far as the eye could see, the fields of corn and sorghum flowed endlessly. A field at this level of productivity was a testament to farming advances and hard work. GPS guided tractors and harvesters had made this entire farm easy for a team of one such as Leroy. Sure it still required some expertise, planning and hard work, but this was beyond what one man could do sixty years ago when Leroy first started plowing fields and planting seeds. Leroy was a few steps ahead of him and looked like he was about to walk right into the field. Tom grabbed his walkie talkie.

"Walter, I'm about to enter the field behind Leroy's house."

"Backups on the way," Walter replied.

"Stand by."

"At first, I thought maybe the seeds I used were too young," Leroy shouted back to Tom as they walked through the browning cornstalks just over Tom's head. Tom shuddered. The first children to go missing were elementary school age.

"You determined that wasn't it then?"

"Seeds wouldn't germinate. So I tried older seeds. They were soft sided, so no reason to scratch the shells."

Tom nodded. The next two kids to go missing were junior high. Typical farm jargon for getting normal seeds with a hard shell to germinate, scratch the shell to allow water to enter and swell the seed.

"But after a few weeks, I still wasn't getting anything. Next batch, I made sure to scratch the shells."

Tom took out his revolver. He could smell the dead bodies. Leroy continued talking. "Still wasn't enough. That's when I thought maybe they just needed a post for the vines to latch onto. That was two weeks ago, but I still haven't seen any sprouting. Could be a bug problem though. There are more flies than I expected."

Leroy walked out into an open area. Tom followed and saw what he was dreading. There were eight dirt mounds, burial sites actually, arrayed in two rows. The furthest row had wooden poles stuck next to the mounds.

"I buried the last seeds deeper. I figured that would help grow a stronger root system." Leroy shook his head. "I still haven't cracked this yet and planting season is damn near over this year."

"Walter, we're about a hundred yards south of the house in the corn field. Let dispatch know and then get down here fast!" Tom said into the walkie talkie.

"Walter doesn't know anything about farming," Leroy said.

Tom pointed his gun at Leroy. "Don't move Leroy. I know this wasn't your fault and it's just the dementia talking."

One of the posts at the end of the rows moved. They both noticed it.

"See, now that's one of the problems I can't figure out. How to keep the damn seeds stationary," Leroy said. He reached down and grabbed a shovel.

"Leroy, stop!"

Leroy didn't listen but headed over to the mound. Tom fired a warning shot into the air. Now both stakes moved. Leroy raised the shovel over his head and was about to swing down on the mound when Tom fired. Leroy dropped the shovel and grabbed his chest where a torrent of blood flowed out. He looked at Tom, still not comprehending what had happened.

Walter rushed into the clearing, gun drawn.

"Son of a bitch, Leroy. Why couldn't you just listen?" Tom said. He holstered his weapon and looked at Walter.

"Cover him."

Tom ran to the shovel, picked it up and began to clear the last two mounds where the two high school aged kids were buried alive.

Thorn in My Side

So that's it then," Daniel said as he pushed the divorce paperwork back to his lawyer. Anna sat still as a tree gazing at him quietly. It always unnerved him when she did that, like she was waiting for an ax to suddenly materialize over his head and drop through his cranium. Perhaps it was just his imagination.

"Well." The young blonde lawyer cleared his throat and pushed another document in front of Daniel.

Daniel looked down and frowned. "The prenup? What about it? She doesn't get anything."

"Actually, do you remember this clause here?" The lawyer pointed at a phrase halfway down the third page of the extensive agreement.

"What, the rose bush thing?"

"If you should die before the rose bush, Anna gets everything."

"That's really more of a will kind of thing, isn't it? Besides, we're not married anymore."

"Dan, remember I advised you not to agree to this five years ago?"

"She doesn't get anything. That was the whole point of the prenup," Daniel smiled.

"Except for this line, legally binding, which actually holds past the end of the marriage and until your death. The bush's DNA is on file."

"If I should die before the rose bush. I'll just cut the damn thing down when I get home."

"Rose bushes grow back fairly quickly. They're hard to kill," the lawyer retrieved the prenup and paged through it again.

"Please don't mess with it," Anna said quietly.

"Oh, now you speak up?" Daniel stood and leaned across the table. "I'm done with you, your funky friends chanting all night, the smell of incense burning all day. I don't need you. I got a nice, pretty new young thing to play with. You're old news, Anna. Throwing you out like the garbage you are."

"Just don't hurt the devil's rose bush."

"Devil's rose bush? I'll cut the fucker down and burn the roots!"

"There's nothing in here saying you cannot dispose of the bush." The lawyer passed the prenup back to Daniel. Daniel picked it up and slammed it on the table in front of Anna.

"It's done, Anna. Divorce is finalized. No more of you and your cronies keeping me up all night. And I will burn that fucking bush to the ground. Then I'll piss on the roots after I dig them up and then I'll burn them too! How's that for a little DNA?"

"Your anger will be the death of you, Daniel," Anna replied calmly.

Daniel stormed out of the room. The lawyer looked after Daniel with concern. Anna just smiled.

Daniel got home and saw his landscaping contractors leaving the property. He jumped out of his car and waved them down. The battered pickup truck came to a halt. Daniel walked up and wrinkled his nose at the smell of the six workers in the truck cab, sweaty from hard work in the sun.

"Miguel," Daniel said to the driver. "I need you to cut down the rose bush."

"*Que?*"

"The rose bush. I need it gone."

"*No habla ingles.*"

"Miguel, you speak perfect English. Get real."

Miguel looked down and shook his head. "No one will go near the rose bush. It's cursed," Miguel said.

"Seriously? It's a bush."

"We have never touched it. That was always Missus Cardonas' treasure. She asked us not to touch it and she would take care of it. One time, my cousin Anthony tried to prune it. He got pricked by one of the thorns and we had to take him to the hospital."

"For a thorn prick?"

"He was in intensive care for two weeks. We won't touch the bush."

"If you don't cut down the bush, you're fired."

Manuel shrugged his shoulders. "It was nice working for you, *señor*," Manuel said and drove off. Daniel watched them drive away dumbfounded.

"She was probably fucking them," he mused and walked back to his car. He drove all the way into the garage, got the huge pruning shears from the wall and set the tool down on the workbench. He took his suit coat off and rolled up his sleeves. He was about to pick up the pruning shears again when he stopped and glanced out the garage door at the bush sitting in front of his porch. It was just a few seconds pause and then he opened a drawer and retrieved a thick pair of leather gardening gloves. He picked up the pruning shears and headed outside.

As the pruning shears bit into the rose bush, Daniel thought he heard a woman screaming. He stopped the tool and looked around. There was no one near. He started the shears up again and continued his work. The strange screaming continued as he cut the bush down. When he had completed stripping it down to nothing more than a trunk, Daniel headed back in and got a small hand ax. With every swing, it sounded like a death gurgle erupted from the bush. Daniel ignored the strange sounds and continued until he'd severed the trunk leaving nothing but a nub sticking out of the ground.

He raked the remains into a pile around the root. He soaked the pile in lighter fluid and threw a lit match on the pile. It went up quickly and burned for several minutes. Daniel noted that the fumes and the plant stunk more than a typical rose bush would.

"You know what that is, Anna? It's the smell of you being out of my fucking life forever!" Daniel shouted to the sky.

When the task was done and every bit of the rose bush had been burned away to his satisfaction, he returned his implements of destruction to the garage. He smiled at the empty spot in front of his porch. He grabbed his suit coat and went in the house. Climbing the stairs to his master bedroom on the second floor, Daniel breathed in the heady smell of no incense burning in his house and smiled. When he got to his room, he tossed the coat on the bed and went into the bathroom to wash his hands and strip out of his clothing. Before he could reach the sink, a wave of excruciating pain overwhelmed him and he fell to the floor screaming in agony. His skin was on fire. When he could finally open his eyes, he looked at his arms and was horrified to find them sliced up and bleeding like he'd been in a fight with a weed eater and lost. Blood soaked through his shirt and pants, leaving a bloody stain on the floor where he fell.

Daniel pulled himself up off the floor and looked in the mirror. Dozens of cuts peppered his face and the blood ran down into his eyes. He turned on the water and grabbed a hand towel. He got it wet and pressed it to his face. The cool wet towel was a relief to his battered flesh and he breathed a sigh of relief even as his tears mixed with the blood.

Daniel pulled the towel tentatively away from his face and was amazed to see there was no blood on the towel. He looked up into the mirror and the cuts were gone. He looked down and there was no blood anywhere. Even the stain on the carpet had disappeared.

"What the fuck?" Daniel whispered. He washed his hands and pulled off his clothes. A wave of exhaustion weighed him down and he fell onto the bed. Darkness weaved its spell and Daniel lapsed into a state of unconsciousness.

Sometime late in the night, Daniel opened his eyes suddenly and looked around. He could move his head, but his limbs weren't responding much. He glanced at them drowsily and saw his wrists bound by thorny vines. An experimental tug on his legs confirmed his suspicion that his feet were similarly bound.

"You've already lost, Daniel. It would be easier for you if you just gave up," Anna said. Daniel turned his head to see her sitting on the night table next to the bed.

"Go to hell," Daniel said. "You're not allowed in this house anymore."

"Who said I was in the house, Daniel? I'm in your mind. I'll be there until the day you die."

"Untie me."

"Those bindings are of your own doing, Daniel," Anna said as she got up and walked to the foot of the bed where Daniel couldn't see her. "And if you're not going to die, I'm afraid you're going to experience a lot more pain."

A searing stabbing pain erupted in Daniel's back. He raised his head and screamed until he was hoarse. The pain continued like a knife being viciously twisted around and around. Daniel tugged and fought with the vines binding his limbs, the thorny ropes digging into his flesh but not releasing him. The intense pain continued for what seemed like hours. Finally, the pain faded away and Daniel collapsed on the bed. His torn body was a road map of pain and torment. Sweat and blood mixed together on his skin and soaked the bed sheets.

Daniel's breath came in shallow gulps. His lungs felt like they were constricting. Panic filled him and he struggled again. The thorny vines on his wrists and legs had disappeared. He got up shakily and looked around the room. His bed was a mess. It looked like a murder had taken place. He looked down at his own body and the cuts from earlier had returned. The gaping wounds oozed blood, but strangely he felt little pain.

Daniel struggled to walk over to the night stand where his cell phone sat. He finally crawled the last few steps and opened the phone. He pressed 911 and pressed the phone to his ear. There was no sound. Daniel pulled the phone away and saw the phone had no service. He dropped to the floor and crawled to the door of his bedroom.

The rest of the house was bathed in cool moonlight. Daniel measured his progress by crawling from moonbeam to moonbeam along the darkened hallway until he reached the top of the stairs. Crawling feet first down the steps was excruciating. The dull pain in his body throbbed and ebbed with each movement. It was as if he felt pain with each heartbeat.

Near the bottom he glanced out at the lawn and saw the most curious thing. There in the moonlight, Anna's rose bush looked as if it had never been cut down and burned. Daniel blinked his amazement. He glanced at the phone near the front door, but rational thought left his mind almost as soon as he saw the rose bush intact and unharmed. There was a basket next to the front door that was full of umbrellas accompanied by a single cane left by an ailing relative years ago. Daniel's rage fueled his body to walk painstaking step after step to reach the cane. He opened the front door and used the cane to support his short walk out to the miraculously restored rose bush.

"I know you're doing this, bitch. I will not give you everything!" Daniel shouted and raised his cane. He struck the rose bush once and a searing burst of light flooded his eyes, driving daggers of pain directly into his brain. Daniel fell to his knees screaming again. His brain felt like it was being torn by two claws lined with thorns. He heard Anna's laughter echoing in the atmosphere as he clawed at his eyes, but couldn't stop the light from entering.

The doctor came into the hospital room and closed the blinds letting in the sunlight.

"His eyes are hypersensitive to the light," Doctor Brown said. He walked over to the morphine drip and saw the flow had been restricted somehow.

"Nurse!"

A harried nurse walked in. She was young and flustered. The middle-aged doctor looked at her and shook his head.

"This man's morphine drip is stuck again. Get a new bag this time."

"Yes, Doctor," she replied and left the room quickly.

Doctor Brown turned to Anna sitting by the window. "I'm sorry, Mrs. Cardona. We'll have this fixed so your husband can pass pain free. I apologize for the inconvenience."

Daniel's lawyer walked up and put his hand on Anna's shoulder. "My sister and I thank you for your understanding and concern, Doctor Brown."

Anna nodded and smiled. Doctor Brown left the room. She looked up at her brother and he smiled at her. "Honestly, Henry. What kind of a fool burns down a rare hybrid wolfs bane and castor rose bush and stands in the smoke breathing in the toxins?"

"What kind of fool indeed, Anna. What kind of fool indeed."

RAIN

Rain is a killer, boys. You can't ever tell with the rain; it can kill you quick, or it can kill you slow, or not at all. They tried to track them killer storms once; all it got them was a stadium full of acid fried fans and two dead football teams. Folks damn near lynched them weathermen for that. I woulda joined 'em if it had been their fault, but it wasn't. It was that damn Mid East maniac; it's really too bad they didn't kill him quicker. He blew the top off of those nuke reactors, throwin' all that radiation into the air. People said it would kill thousands all over the world for the next couple thousand years.

I get real mad sometimes, thinking about the whole thing. That Mid East bastard killed my mom, ya know. She got caught out in one of them rainstorms that kills ya slow. That's not the half of it; she was two months along with my little brother Joey in her belly. She died nine years later; her skin was half rotted away from the cancer. I think she mighta tried to hang on a while longer if it hadn't a been for what happened to Joey.

Little Joey, ya see, never grew up. He grew just like a normal kid except for he never stood taller than twenty-two inches. Everyone called him 'Little Joey;' I don't think he minded it too much. He never liked for anyone to pick on him, though, and that's what started all the trouble.

Mom was in the hospital again; this time for good. Joey had just turned eight. I was working here at the grocery store to help with the bills. On that particular day, I was working in the back, moving all the stock around. Joey was out in front of our house, piling up some stones into a castle. One of the local gangs was walkin' by and spotted Joey. Leader was a young brat named Stace. Well, Stace thought it'd be a real hoot to tie Joey up to one of those aluminum pallets they use for cargo shipping on the docks down the street. So, Stace and the gang grabbed Joey and tied him to a pallet; then they hauled it halfway up a street light right in front of our house. Joey was plenty scared; he didn't know what the gang was going to do to him. They just stood around laughing, though. That didn't worry Joey so much; he was used to it.

Then the sky got dark, and somebody yelled 'Killer rain!' Everybody ran for cover, but no one thought to stop for a few seconds to let Joey down. They left him hanging there for the killer rain. Joey was hysterical; he kept yellin' for someone to let him down. As he was screamin' for help, the rain started come down to the left of him. Steam or smoke, Joey didn't know which, was rising from the wet street. Then Joey screamed like he was dyin'; the rain was fallin' on him. One of the neighbors, Hank, heard him and ran to the window; he told me those gang rats all covered their ears and shut their eyes. Joey stopped screaming after a couple seconds. When the rain stopped, the gang just ran, never looking back to see if Joey was still alive.

Hank ran from his house when the rain stopped and let Joey down. Joey was fine physically, but his eyes just stared ahead at nothing. Hank took Joey into our house and laid him down on his bed. Then he called me.

When I got home, we went in to look at Joey; he was gone. A few days later, the guys in Stace's gang started showin' up dead; two tiny hands had crushed their windpipes. The last three got wise and wore protective collars. They also carried all the weapons they could get their hands on. It didn't matter, though; Joey got two of them in one night. He left Stace for last. Stace got spooked and left town. He was two whole states away when Joey got him; chased him out of a building right into a killer rain. Stace hung on for a few hours after the rain stopped; Joey stood just out of reach, watching him die slowly. He was screamin', and cryin', and all his skin was just falling off. If ya ask me, that's justice, boys. Don't ever pick on someone else; it can come back to haunt ya.

Joey comes by and visits when he can. Cops are still looking for him, but they'll never catch him. He still gets that haunted look in his eyes when it rains. Mom died a few days after we got word that Stace was dead. I think she was glad Joey killed them. I figure she would've done it herself, if she could've.

Rain's stopped. I better get back to work. Wouldn't do for me to lose my job; Joey's tenth birthday is next month, and I got a great present planned for him. I'm gonna buy him a good umbrella.

You kids run along and watch out for the rain.

HANKY CRANKY

orey looked over the menu and smirked. The prices were outrageous but well within his means. He looked up over the menu at the bar and saw the blonde he'd been tracking for days still nursing her martini. The waiter showed up at his table and Morey almost snarled, but kept his composure and ordered a glass of 2003 Chateau Lafite-Rothschild. No reason to skimp on the evening's meal—he would celebrate ahead of time and then perhaps again tomorrow. Tonight, he would capture his quarry.

In the middle of his Ayam Cemani Chicken dish, the woman he'd been watching left the bar, leaving behind a half drunk martini and a small pile of cash. Morey sniffed in annoyance at the half eaten dish and sighed. He took one last drink of his wine, plopped down several hundred dollar bills and left the table. Staying just a few hundred yards behind her, Morey followed the statuesque blonde out of the restaurant and for several blocks until she went down into the subway.

After a quick jog down the steps into the subway, he watched from afar as she got onto the train he knew she would. She was heading home. He smiled and returned topside. He slipped on a pair of gloves; it was just nippy enough to justify, but he did it to reduce the likelihood of leaving any evidence behind during his hunt. After a brief wait, he grabbed a cab and gave the cabby the address a block away from hers.

The cabby tried to start up a conversation, but Morey tossed him a hundred and told him "best speed and as quietly as you can." The cabby shut up and sped to their destination at a breakneck pace, causing Morey to raise his eyebrows at some of the shortcuts the cabby took that he hadn't considered before. As they arrived, he tossed him another hundred and thanked him for taking him home.

The cabby gave a little whoop and drove off. Morey watched until the taxi turned a corner and then walked the block to his quarry's residence. He took out a key duplicate he'd been able to get made of her door lock—same key for the deadbolt as the normal lock. That was the kind of laziness that made his hobby that much easier.

He looked at his watch. She'd be there within fifteen minutes as the subway train traveled. He marveled at how she took the time and expense to go out to a bar when she worked two jobs just to keep this townhome in the Bronx. He'd worked out the salary she'd need from the legal secretary job she kept during the day and the part-time bookkeeper work she parlayed during the weekends and odd evenings. He mused there must be some off book work she did online to keep the expenses at bay, but he hardly understood the need. She was alone, no family that he could find and no acquaintances that he could discern during the time and expense he'd taken to look into her affairs. She was a perfect mark for his needs. Anyone who led a lonely existence was his for the taking and, to his mind, was in need of relief from such a dismal existence.

While he'd tested the keys before and found no alarm, he'd merely taken a quick peek at the layout before leaving just a few days ago. He hadn't taken the time to observe the surroundings much.

From his vantage point in the shadows of the living room, he observed the curious decorations on her mantelpiece and walls. He recognized some rare and expensive items from the Ivory Coast and different places on the African continent—masks and ritualistic pieces that seemed a mystery to him even with his extensive collection of antiques and curiosities. It was a shame he couldn't study them at more length. Perhaps he'd be able to pick some of them up at the public auction after her body was discovered and the investigation into her disappearance and death came to a dead end.

When she put her keys into the lock, he nearly stiffened up, which could have caused sound, alerting his quarry to his presence. He calmed his nerves and waited for her to lock the door behind her and hang her coat up in the closet. She walked into the kitchen, setting her keys and phone on the counter as anticipated.

The surprise was when the panels slid quietly into place across the windows in the living room. Morey heard other things sliding in a barely discernible scratching along hidden rails and then clicking nearly silently into place. The lights came on and flooded the room with light.

"Took you long enough, Morey," the blonde said as she strolled into the room, dropping her dress to the woven rug with a curious pattern reminiscent of Zulu art Morey had seen on display at auctions a dozen times. He'd never picked any up, but he was familiar with the style. Morey looked up at the blonde as she smiled at him. "I was going mad with hunger waiting for to make your appearance in my humble abode."

"Hunger? I'm afraid it's you that has made the miscalculation, my dear," Morey said, observing her naked form and seeing she had no weapons. Was she going to fuck him to death? "I'll carve the succulent flesh from your lithe form and drink in your screams."

Morey took a step forward and then hesitated. The blonde's skin began to darken and mutate as feathers formed. Her head became misshapen and formed a beak topped by glowing blue eyes. Her arms lengthening and her hands curled into black tipped claws. Lightening arced out from her claws as a full set of black wings unfolded behind her. The lightning struck Morey, knocking him backward into the wall.

Morey's eyes fluttered open and he tried to move. He found himself strapped to a gurney in a basement. He assumed it was a basement due to the rafters he observed above him. He turned his head and noted a panel similar to the one he'd seen in his quarry's living room covering the windows there. He tried to open his mouth, but noted it had been sewn shut.

He looked down at his arm and saw an IV coming from his arm. He wrinkled his nose and felt something tickling his nostril. He realized he had a tube running through his nasal cavity and down into his throat.

He heard footsteps coming down the staircase and looked over to see the blonde once again, now dressed in a surgical smock. She had a mask as well, but it was pulled down.

"My last feast was a homeless man who tried to rob me as I walked to my day job, you know, at the law firm. I escaped his attack, of course. I tracked him for a few days until I noted a predatory pattern on random pedestrians. He did it to support a drug habit, of course. I took him in the middle of the night while he was in the process of a meth purchase. I took the dealer as well. The dealer didn't partake of his product, so his blood was cleaner and definitely more delicious."

The blonde bent over and manipulated something under the table. Morey heard liquid dripping into a glass and he imagined the wine he'd consumed at the restaurant... was it last night? She stood up and held a wine glass half full with blood red liquid. She raised it to him, then took a mouthful of the liquid and swallowed it. She closed her eyes and took in a deep breath.

"Oh, you have taken care of yourself, Morey," she said and walked over to the panel. She touched the edge and it opened a sliver. Daylight streamed through the opening. She held the glass up to the light and admired the quality of the light shining through it. "The dealer sadly had some sort of heart condition, so he died fairly quickly. He didn't take very well to the milking process, I'm afraid. The addict, well, he lasted weeks. Although that was a relief to my process, it was only near the end that his blood started to taste normal having been flushed of the toxins he had injected himself with. He was at his purest detoxified self when his liver, of all things, gave out and his blood became less than optimal. I had to let him go much earlier than planned. I'd only just caught your eye."

Morey attempted to shout, trying to get the attention of a passerby. The woman chuckled at his muffled outburst.

"Oh Morey, don't put yourself into such distress. We're not in the Bronx anymore. You won't be getting anyone's attention out here at the estate. I do have a gardener come by once a week, but I'll make sure you're well under lock and key whenever someone comes by. I just thought you might enjoy a little light during your stay. You'll be here quite a while. I will so enjoy your contribution to my health."

She raised her glass and drained it.

"I'm sure you're wondering how a vampire can stand the sunlight," she said as she pointed to the window. "But then, you tracked me walking around in the daylight as well as the night, so you know I can't possibly be a vampire. I'm an impundulu. Ancient really. I outlived the tribe and string of umthakathi I had served. Left to my own devices, I had to make due. When white encroachers slaughtered my food source, I decided to relocate and take advantage of Caucasian ignorance of the unknown. You'll never believe the length people will go to trying to explain away something they've seen with their own eyes."

She set the glass down on the steps and walked over to Morey. She caressed his cheek. "Do you know they call me the Mothman in West Virginia? Delightfully ignorant and superstitious, the human race is endlessly entertaining."

Morey squirmed and realized the extent of his captivity. His legs, arms and even hands were securely strapped down with padded restraints.

"It is hard, isn't it Morey? Being the prey instead of the hunter? Oh, I almost forgot the best part of my hunting process. When I find a rich asshole like you, my work at the law firm is most helpful. I'll be slowly transferring your assets while you're hopping across the globe. Well, that's what the digital trail will show anyway. When the time comes, I fancy you disappearing during a fishing trip in Bali or perhaps a hiking trip in the Amazon? Yes, I like the Amazon. Reminds me of home."

She smiled at him as she reached over his head and pulled a mask down over has nose and mouth.

"Now I'll just put you to sleep for a little while. Can't have you freaking out and damaging yourself."

Morey heard a light squeaking sound and smelled a sweet scent flood his senses.

"There you go. Now just count to..."

Bully For You

 ennis closed the folder and looked across the table at Mister Bhandari. The Indian man's jaw and fists were both clenched.

"Mister Crenshaw," the man to Dennis' right began in a heavy Indian accent. "You didn't have to be here for the closing of the case."

"Oh, I know," Dennis replied as he stood up. "I just wanted Mister Bhandari here to see who had taken everything from him. Perhaps a cautionary tale to those who might cross me in the future."

"You've taken everything from my family!" Mister Bhandari shouted as he stood up. "You will be cursed for your greed and viciousness!"

"Oh I've done more than take everything from you, Mister Bhandari," Dennis said with a grin. "After everything is liquidated, I think you'll still face many fines from the state and local government. Even bankruptcy can't get you out of some of those. Good luck."

Mister Bhandari's lawyers held him back from physically attacking Dennis as he left the room.

Dennis climbed into the back of the black SUV. He smiled at his driver and nodded.

"Another successful steal, Mr. Crenshaw?" the Indian driver asked as he pulled away from the curb.

"Deal, Faqid. Another successful deal." Dennis chuckled as he looked out the window. "It's a combination of what you know and who you know. Now, let's explore this little thirty thousand acres I've bought in the middle of nowhere."

Outside the window, Dennis observed the squalor and poverty rampant in this area of the country. He shook his head. "So much wasted potential on these streets, Faqid."

"India has advantages of population and disadvantages of population," Faqid replied. "You're not the first person who's been dismayed by the poverty."

"Useless international watchdogs protect these people from working. They sit around unproductive when they could be producing garments, electronics, or any number of consumer goods by the truckload."

"You would see them living better?" Faqid asked as he steered around some carts in the road.

"Oh heavens, no. I'd exploit the workers or the land or both for my profit. I doubt their day to day living would improve much, but at least they'd be productive. For the good of all humanity and my bank accounts of course."

"Of course, sir," Faqid replied, but seemed less enthusiastic.

They drove on for another hour as the number of people on the road dwindled down to just a scattered few here and there, mostly just resting under the shade of a tree. Finally, they took a turn down a dirt road and reached an armed checkpoint. Dennis got out and walked up confidently to the armed gunmen at the gate. These men were American with crew cuts and military style uniforms.

A younger Indian man in a suit walked out of a small shack off to the side of the road. Dennis nodded his head to the man.

"Mister Bhandari, good to see you again," Dennis said.

"I trust everything went well with my father?" the Indian man said.

"I've already wired your payment," Dennis replied. "Now, let's talk a walk to discuss the other information."

The two men ventured further onto the property a few hundred yards away from the checkpoint. The armed men seemed to pay them no mind as they scanned the area outside the property.

Dennis looked around at the thick forest on either side of the rough road. He was less concerned about parabolic eavesdropping than a building being bugged. He felt relatively safe at this point.

"You mentioned treasure as the real reason your father wanted to secure this property," Dennis said.

"A fool's errand, I believe, but one that caught your interest nonetheless," the Indian man replied. "I have no interest in such foolishness, but you wanted the stories just the same."

He looked around at the forest and nodded. "I've often felt ill at ease here, but my father has long been a guardian of this space and he revered it. It's said the yaksa or yaksi guard immense wealth below, but such is their ferocity, it can't be retrieved by mortal man," he chuckled. "Before my father took over this forest, there were tales of men by the hundreds facing their end in the darkness here. I suspect they simply ran afoul of natural predators and dangers, but there are numerous tales of fanciful deaths. That's pretty much the totality of the tales as my father related them to me during my childhood. I took them to be tales to scare children, but when I turned twelve, he refused to speak of it further after…"

He faltered in his speech and swallowed hard. "My uncle sought the treasure for himself, a singularly selfish pursuit. One day he took my brother Aarush into the forest to seek it out. They never returned." He looked down the road into the property and seemed lost in his memories.

"Well, I'll just bring in some prospectors with equipment and we'll see what we can find," Dennis said. "We'll dig it up when we locate it. No treasure is ever lost forever."

The Indian man smiled grimly at Dennis. "This road was built by hand, Mister Crenshaw. Many men labored months to put it in place. Machinery wouldn't run. No electronics or engines of any kind make it more than a few feet past the edge of the forest before they cease to operate. They tow them out with ropes and the machinery functions again outside the boundaries of the forest," he said as he shrugged his shoulders. "I wish you luck in your search. Perhaps you will find what no one could before. Perhaps you'll get your mining operation to function here. Perhaps you'll perish as so many have before you."

"Well, I won't be dissuaded by folk tales and superstitions," Dennis said confidently. "If there's treasure here, I'll find it."

The Indian man turned and walked away without looking back. Dennis watched him go and when the man stepped past the gate, a sound caused Dennis to turn back to the forest. He could've sworn he heard giggling. He looked all around, but couldn't see anyone or anything out of the ordinary.

"You're playing games with the wrong millionaire, whoever you are," Dennis murmured. He walked back to the men at the gate.

"Burton, the others arrive soon?" Dennis asked the older man with the black beret.

"They'll be here first thing tomorrow," Burton reported.

"Good. I think we'll be taking a little expedition into the woods when they arrive. Be sure they're well provisioned for a journey into the forest."

Dennis sat down at the dinner table and the house manservant, Hiranga, brought out the first courses of the meal. Dennis looked it over and smiled.

"This will do nicely. Dismissed," Dennis said as he picked up his utensils. Hiranga left the room. Dennis ate the first few bites of his meal when he noticed Hiranga standing at the other side of the room watching him.

"Hiranga, you were dismissed."

Hiranga walked lazily around the table until he was standing next to Dennis. "Tell, me, Mister Crenshaw, what are your plans for the forest?"

"I'll do whatever I damn well please with my forest. You're fired, Hiranga. Get out. Now," Dennis went back to eating his meal.

When he looked up from his meal, Hiranga floated in midair across the room in a seated position.

"What the hell?" Dennis stood up and slammed his utensils down.

When Hiranga raised his head, his eyes glowed with a purple shimmer. "You should not harm the forest or the grounds. It is sacred and will be protected," Hiranga said. He smiled and long fangs appeared to protrude from his upper canines.

"I'll cut the forest down and plunder it as I see fit—it's mine now!"

From behind Dennis, the sound of plates dropping and shattering on the floor drew his attention. He turned around to see Hiranga looking with fear at the floating figure. Hiranga screamed and fled the room.

Dennis turned back to look where the floating figure had been but he was gone. "I'll not be dissuaded by some stupid parlor tricks!" Dennis shouted.

He looked down at the spilled food and broken dishes. "I've lost my appetite anyway," he said and stormed out of the dining room.

The next morning, twenty men were assembled and waiting with various equipment at hand including metal detectors and firearms. Backpacks were filled with provisions as well, even though there were only forty-six square miles of forest to explore. Dennis stepped out of his vehicle dressed in khaki clothing, boots and a hat with mosquito netting on it. He walked over to Burton.

"Excellent preparation. Are we ready to proceed?" Dennis asked.

"I'll be personally escorting you with ten men. The others will patrol the perimeter."

"You have the drones I requested?" Dennis asked.

"Umm..." Burton shifted his footing. "They ceased to function just a few feet into the perimeter of the property."

"All of them?"

"We sent in ten of the twenty drones we have. All ten went down. We've kept the remaining ones outside the property scanning the perimeter from there."

"Well, they're GPS and radio not cell, right?"

"We retrieved them and they appeared to be completely knocked out until we got them to the edge of the forest when they resumed function. Well, what was left of them resumed function. Most of them were damaged from the fall."

Dennis looked around at the forest and scratched his head. "I cleared it with the government. There are no clandestine military activities within the borders of this forest. There should be no jamming equipment of any kind. We may be dealing with a rogue force operating here illegally. Keep your weapons handy. We may face resistance we haven't anticipated."

Burton went over to his group and barked out orders as the men gathered up their equipment and assembled on the road inside the gate. Dennis walked further up the road into the forest with his cell phone in his hand. He watched in frustration as he didn't just lose signal but his phone completely shut off. He pressed the button on the radio on his lapel.

"Burton, this is Crenshaw, over." He let go of the button and didn't even get static. There was no response from the leader of the mercenaries. From somewhere in the forest, Dennis heard the same laugh as he had the day before. He turned sharply and looked in the direction of the laugh and thought he saw a brief glimmer of purple reminiscent of Hiranga floating in the air yesterday.

He clenched his jaw and walked back to the group of men waiting to head out. "Somebody is toying with us, gentlemen. Let's be sure our weapons are ready to show them what we think of trespassers."

The men surreptitiously glanced at Burton who gave a nearly imperceptible nod. Dennis sighed, but didn't say anything. He paid Burton well to supply the muscle he needed; if that meant his men looked to Burton for direction, Dennis wasn't going to begrudge Burton the respect of his men. Discipline could be the difference between life and death out here.

He walked up to Burton and bent his head down.

"Just to be clear, an EMP is a burst, not a consistent field being generated, correct?" Dennis whispered.

"There's shielding to encompass an enclosure and limited distance electromagnetic dampening systems, but nothing of the scale to cover an entire forest. Surely it can't be an issue throughout the entire property; that would take a massive power source and, I'll be honest, I've never heard of anything on that scale," Burton whispered back.

"I think we'll have communication issues inside, so perhaps a tighter formation would be prudent," Dennis said. "There's something at play. Perhaps it's a natural occurrence like a large magnetic meteorite or something in the center of the property. It's not outside the realm of possibility."

"That, Mister Crenshaw, would certainly be something someone might want to keep hidden." Burton smiled. "We'll clear this forest one acre at a time if we have to."

"Good man," Dennis replied.

"Heads up, men," Burton announced. "We're going to keep a tight formation. Radio communication appears to be inoperable within the forest. Keep your eyes open. No hostiles confirmed, but anything is possible. Let's head out."

Burton turned around and headed into the forest via the dirt road followed closely by Dennis and the rest of the mercenary force.

When they reached the end of the dirt road, the thick brush made progress slow. Within fifteen minutes, they could no longer see the road behind them. Ten minutes after that, they all heard the strange laughter within the forest that Dennis had heard twice before.

One of the men shouted out in surprise and there was a huge sound of branches breaking accompanied by a fading scream.

"Something just threw Billings hundreds of feet behind us," one of the men reported.

"Visual?" Burton barked back.

"Nothing," came the reply.

"There may be booby traps of some kind," Burton called out. "Anson and Mowry, go find Billings. Triage, medevac if necessary, then report back."

"Booby traps?" Dennis asked.

"Got a better explanation?" Burton replied.

They continued moving forward until another scream that faded even quicker than the first.

"Greg?!" one of the other men shouted. "Shit, they got Greg! He went straight up!"

They all converged on where Greg had disappeared.

"He was just behind me!" a ginger haired soldier reported.

"Look up in the treetops," Burton said. "He may have gotten snagged by a snare."

They all looked up and that's when they heard the screaming of Greg's return as he fell toward them. They all jumped back and Greg hit the floor of the forest with a sickening, wet thud. The red haired mercenary ran up to Greg and immediately turned away and vomited. Burton and Dennis approached the fallen soldier.

Greg's skull was split open with brain matter and blood sprayed around in a three foot radius. Several of his limbs were clearly broken where the body had impacted the ground. Burton sighed.

"Smitty and Greg served together in the field for years. Pretty sure this wasn't how they thought it would end." Burton shook his head. "I sure didn't think it would end like this."

"What is happening?" Dennis asked.

"I don't know and that's why we're falling back," Burton said.

"What? We have to confront this thing and secure the grounds!" Dennis shouted.

"We're not securing anything if we're all dead, Mister Crenshaw. We need to regroup and come at this differently," Burton said calmly and turned to two of the remaining personnel. "Bag him up. We're not leaving him here. Best speed."

The two men broke out a body bag, put on gloves and began to quickly put Greg in the bag carefully. Burton walked around them and put a hand on Smitty's back as the younger man continued heaving.

"This is bullshit!" Dennis shouted as he walked away from the men zipping up the body bag. "I didn't pay you assholes to be pansies at the first sign of danger!"

Then Dennis disappeared. There wasn't even a scream.

Burton stood up and turned around. He walked over to where Dennis had been standing and noticed the ground there had a consistency similar to quicksand.

"Well," Burton said as he turned back to his men. "I guess it's a good thing we got paid fifty percent up front. Let's finish this up and get back to base camp."

The men hurried about their activities and exited the forest as quickly as they could, facing no further obstacles or dangers.

Dennis awoke on top of a pile of gold, rubies and various types of jewelry. He picked up a handful of coins and laughed.

"Yes!" Dennis shouted as he sat up. His shout echoed for several seconds. Dennis looked up and realized he was in an underground cavern. The ceiling was thirty feet high and the walls seemed even further across winding away into multiple passages.

Oh look, it's awake, a feminine voice said in his head.

How should we punish it before we consume it? another voice said in his head.

As Dennis looked around in bewilderment, two nearly ten foot tall women with full breasts and hips came out of one of the passages. They had a few wisps of shimmering cloth strewn about their bodies, but the scant garments did little to cover their almost nude bodies.

Let it decide, the first voice said as the first woman stopped in front of him and looked at the second. The second one nodded.

Dennis looked around him and found a long slender scepter. He picked it up and it seemed rather hefty. He swung it in front of him between the two huge women.

"Stand back! I claim this treasure in the name of Dennis Crenshaw!" Dennis shouted at the two women. They raised their eyebrows in response to his declaration and then grinned, revealing the same canine teeth he had seen on Hiranga floating in his dining room the previous evening.

Oh look, he has chosen! The first one pointed at the scepter.

Do you think he will break as easily as the others? the second voice asked and the second woman looked at the first curiously.

Dennis looked back and forth between the two women, waving the scepter and shouting. The first woman moved her hand incredibly fast and caught the scepter in her hand, wrenching it from his grip. Her other hand reached out and grabbed his head. Dennis wriggled around and punched the hand with his hands, but her grip was like stone. She could've crushed his head, but she applied just enough pressure to keep hold of his head and render him essentially helpless.

Dennis felt cold bits of what seemed like metal gliding across his skin. He felt his clothing being cut and pulled from his body, leaving him naked except for his socks and boots. He shivered as he felt the cool air of the cavern hit his bare skin.

The first woman removed her hand from his head as the second one grabbed his legs and turned him around and slammed him face first into the pile of gold and jewels. He felt a hand press against his upper back, immobilizing him once again. Two hands pulled his legs apart. Dennis wrenched his head around and he saw the scepter being moved between his legs.

"No! Please! I'll give you anything! I'm very rich!" Dennis screamed.

It's very loud, the second voice said.

Didn't it say it wanted treasure? the first voice asked.

Yet it's rich. What could it possibly do with more treasure than it has? the second voice pondered.

I know! Let's give it more treasure! the first voice said excitedly.

They turned Dennis over and the second woman held him down.

The first woman set down the scepter and picked up a large gem a little larger than Dennis fist. She squeezed his mouth open and shoved the gem into his mouth, breaking teeth and his jaw in the process. Dennis felt blood and chunks of his broken teeth trickling to the back of his throat, causing him to cough amidst his screams of agony.

Still noisy, the first voice said.

Perhaps one of these fine silk bags over its head will help? the second voice offered.

Yes, let's try that before we give him his treasure of first choice, the first voice agreed. The first woman rummaged around in the piles of treasure and came up with an ornate silk bag. She placed it over Dennis head and drew the drawstring tight. Dennis found it incredibly hard to breath.

Next he felt his body flipped over again and the process repeated until he felt the metal shaft of the scepter against his inner thighs. He struggled in vain before he felt indescribably pain rip through his lower torso and felt the warm trickle of his bodily fluids leaking all around him. He screamed and grasped at the treasure beneath his shaking hands, worthless to a dead man.

No, they are still very fragile. Quickly now, we don't want to lose too much of this deliciousness, the first voice said.

I'm so hungry! the second voice agreed.

Dennis felt his broken body get lifted into the air and two sets of fangs dig deep into his flesh. The last thing he heard were slurping sounds as they began to drain his body of blood.

DOG EAT DOG WORLD

Pablo dropped the bloody pipe wrench on the ground and looked at the pile of hair and flesh that used to be a live animal moments ago. He turned to look at the barking dogs behind the chain link fence.

"Do not show weakness!" he shouted at the animals. They were in individual pens, jumping at the chain link as they aggressively tried to close the gap between them and their handler.

"Hey Pablo," another man said as he poked his head through a steel door. "Clean up and take out the trash. DQ is on his way to discuss our losses."

"Shit," Pablo said. "I'm on it."

The steel door slammed shut and Pablo rested his hand on the cinderblock wall. He looked at the spray of blood up on the cinderblock and pooling around the dead animal slowing trickling toward the drain in the center of the large room.

He walked by the line of barking dogs, pit bulls for the most part, and retrieved a wheelbarrow from outside. He stopped at the utility closet on the way back in and grabbed a set of thick black rubber gloves. He pulled them on and pushed the wheelbarrow next to the pile of broken flesh on the ground. He grabbed the torso of the animal and pulled it up into the wheelbarrow with a grunt.

He wheeled the wheelbarrow to the other end of the dog pens and down a hallway to a separate room with another steel door. He propped the door open and pushed the wheelbarrow inside. He pressed a button on the wall and listened to the burners kick on inside the incinerator just a few steps away. He took the thick gloves off his hands and set them on the wheelbarrow handles. He gave a heavy sigh.

He left the incinerator room and walked back up to the front room. The dogs continued to bark maniacally at him.

"Shut up!" he shouted and a few of them backed down for a moment, but then returned to the frenzy as the others continued their overzealous aggression. Pablo giggled.

He walked over to the wash basin and pulled out the thick industrial water hose. He turned the spigot it was attached to and the hose got thick with water pressure. He picked up the nozzle and began to spray down the bloody walls and floor, sending the blood, fur and bits of canine tooth hurtling toward the floor drain. When he'd taken care of most of it, he noticed he'd probably have to scrub to get the rest of it off the walls.

"Dammit," Pablo murmured. He got a grin and turned the cold water onto the barking dogs. They continued their barking frenzy.

"You're a bunch of ugly mutts, you know that?" he shouted at them as he mentally catalogued every scar, open wound, missing ear and damaged eye of the fighting dogs under his care.

He got tired of the water play, put the hose back by the wash basin and grabbed a thick scrub brush. He sprayed some detergent on the blood stains on the walls and floor and started scrubbing. Ten minutes later, he finished and sprayed off the cleaned surfaces. There was nary a trace left of the horrific violence he'd perpetrated there just half an hour earlier.

He put the hose back again, turned off the water and went back down the hall to the incinerator room. He slid his gloves back on and opened the incinerator door to pull out the slotted tray. He hefted the dead dog onto the tray and slid the tray back into the incinerator, closing the heavy door with a slam. He dropped the locking bar into place.

"Adios Fluffy," he said to the incinerator. He grabbed the wheelbarrow and pushed it back down the hall. He stopped to clean it out and rinsed everything down the floor drain. Satisfied that all was clean, he picked up the wheelbarrow to move it when the entire building began to shake.

Before Pablo could reach the door to take shelter, a chunk of the ceiling fell on his head, knocking him unconscious.

Pablo awoke with a splitting headache and excruciating pain radiating up his left leg. He pushed himself up off the floor but couldn't move from the spot. He looked back and saw his left leg was pinned by a section of collapsed cinder block wall and bits of the roof.

Smoke and heat came from the area where the dogs were housed. He looked toward the animal pens and saw the building was in flames. He realized the earthquake must've ruptured a gas line and the burning incinerator had lit it on fire. Just beyond the smoke rising from the debris, he saw a column of flame rising into the air.

"Hello?" Pablo shouted out. There was no answer.

The dog fighting kennel was in the middle of an abandoned industrial warehouse district shut down years ago by wildfires. Pablo's employers had gotten the entire land cheap since it was uninsurable due to the wildfire danger in combination with the earthquake risk after a new fault had been identified close by. There were no neighbors and his co-worker was the only other person on site; that guy provided the muscle in case anyone came to steal the dogs. Pablo called out again, but there was no answer from his accomplice, so he had to assume he was similarly injured or had abandoned the building without him. No honor among thieves.

Then Pablo heard a growl. He looked quickly at the pens and that was when he noticed the chain link fence had been compromised. He could make out one dog trapped beneath some rubble. It wasn't moving and was likely dead. He glanced around the ruined building, but couldn't see any other dogs until he noticed one atop the rubble looking down at him.

Diablo was the oldest surviving fighting dog and the most vicious. He looked at Pablo with a hunter's glare. Five more dogs topped the rubble next to Diablo. They glanced down at Pablo, but didn't seem to be as intent upon him as they were distracted by the cacophony of sounds and smells around them.

Pablo looked around and saw the pipe wrench he'd used earlier. He reached out and grabbed the end of it which was stuck under another collapsed wall. It wouldn't budge.

Diablo growled again. Pablo looked up at him and scowled.

Don't show fear, he thought.

Pablo looked at his trapped leg and used his other one to push against the debris and pull his shattered limb from under the rubble. He screamed throughout the ordeal. When he finally got it out, he rolled onto his side and pushed himself against the wall. He got up into a seated position. Sweat poured down his face. He got dizzy for a moment and shook his head to keep himself awake.

He heard movement overhead and looked up. Nearly every dog he'd spent the years training, beating, yelling at, and teasing them through the chain link fence was now looking down at him. Pablo counted eleven dogs in total. Including the dead dog he'd just incinerated and the one killed by the falling debris, that made thirteen. Two were still missing.

Except for Diablo, the others didn't seem that interested in him. He wondered if they couldn't navigate the debris to get to him. It seemed pretty straightforward to him, but these dogs hadn't had a normal upbringing. They lived in pens and fought in rings. Rinse, repeat, again and again and again until they were too damaged to fight. Then, it was up to Pablo to put them down.

There was more movement above and the other dogs seemed to get excited. Then Pablo saw Rocky emerge from between the dogs with something in his mouth that looked like a ball. Rocky dropped the ball and it tumbled down the wall of debris until it rolled into Pablo's leg.

Pablo looked down at the ball and realized it was covered in blood, hair and flesh. With a shaking hand still enclosed in the thick rubber glove, he reached out to the ball and moved it around. His bodyguard, Chico Ramirez, looked up at him from empty eye sockets in a bloody face, skin torn by canine teeth. Chico's two gold front teeth poked out from the broken jaw.

Rocky barked happily from the top of the debris wall. Diablo answered by snapping angrily at Rocky who backed away.

"Eh, maybe you will tear each other apart before you worry about me," Pablo whispered and laughed.

Diablo growled and Pablo saw the heavily scarred Rottweiler pit bull mix looking directly at him again. Pablo grabbed the end of the wrench again. This time with a better leverage point, he was able to get it free from the debris. He held it in his hands like an old friend.

"Huh?!" he shouted at Diablo. "You want to mess with me, you get the pipe!"

Every dog now looked at Pablo. They all growled. Rocky took the first tentative steps down the piles of broken building. Pablo reached over and grabbed a broken chunk of cinder block and hurled it at Rocky, striking the dog in the rib cage. Rocky yelped and stopped where he was.

"Get out of here!" Pablo yelled at Rocky.

The other dogs got quiet as they watched Rocky. The injured dog finished its descent and stepped onto the debris ridden floor mere steps away from Pablo's feet.

Pablo swung the wrench through the air in front of him. Rocky stood where he was and looked down at Pablo's ruined leg. He cocked his head and looked up at Pablo again. Suddenly, the dog darted forward and grabbed Pablo's broken foot in its teeth and violently shook its head back and forth. Pablo cried out in anger and pain. He swung the wrench at Rocky, but missed. He kicked his foot and connected with Rocky's head, but the animal acted like he hadn't even been touched and continued violently wrenching Pablo broken foot.

Rocky tugged at the broken limb and started pulling Pablo away from the wall. Pablo leaned forward in a desperate attempt to fight the dog off and managed to connect with the wrench, knocking Rocky backward a few feet. Rocky stumbled a few times and then fell to the ground. His chest moved up and down, so he still clung to life, but he didn't appear to be conscious anymore.

Diablo gave a loud bark and the other dogs began to descend the walls of debris. They got down to the bottom and assembled around Rocky, nudging the unresponsive animal with their noses. Diablo reached the bottom and stepped forward with a growl. The other dogs turned around and formed a semi-circle around Pablo.

Pablo swung the wrench in a low arc around him, warding off the dogs. But with each pass he made with the hated weapon, the growls from the assembled pack grew louder.

"I'm not going anywhere without a fight, perros miserable!" Pablo shouted.

Diablo barked once and the dogs attacked as one. Pablo swung the wrench once more before two dogs latched onto his rubber gloved hand and bit through the material, tearing into the flesh of his right arm. Two dogs tore into his ruined leg while two more attacked his good leg.

Three dogs whipped their heads back and forth on his left arm, tearing off fingers and chunks of flesh. Blood soaked the dusty floor of the destroyed building. Two dogs tore at Pablo's abdomen, opening him up like a can. His intestines spilled onto his lap as Diablo jumped in the middle of the fray and latched its powerful jaws around Pablo's throat and tore it out, whipping its head back and forth in a vicious fury.

As blood spilled out his torn jugular vein, the last thing Pablo saw was Diablo tearing into his face and ripping out his left eye.

THE SYSTEM

organ watched the smoke rising from the barrel of the gun in slow motion. The cry of pain from Jeremy just a few feet away seemed to come to him through ear plugs. It stretched out low and slow for several seconds. His eyes rose from the barrel to see the young man he'd just shot clutching his chest as he went to his knees. Morgan looked back down at the gun in wonder.

Ten years ago, he'd done his first snatch and grab, running off with an old woman's purse and delivering it to his new gang just a few blocks away. His cut of the old woman's money had been ten bucks. It seemed like a bonanza to him at the tender age of ten. Crazy to think how his appetites had grown beyond running down to the corner store and buying a soda and a sandwich.

The woman had filed a police report and one of his fellow gang members had been caught trying to use her credit card. The gang had responded by tracking the old woman to her home, killing her and torching her little apartment. The fire had taken half the building down and killed another three people who couldn't escape the apartment with faulty smoke detectors, no fire extinguishers and a broken fire hydrant across the street. But Morgan had gotten his ten dollars.

"It's the system," the gang leader had told him. "It's trying to hold you down, you gotta fight back."

The gang leader was dead by the time Morgan turned twelve, a victim of a turf war between rival gangs. It wasn't even Morgan's gang involved; they just got caught in the crossfire one day. By the time the smoke cleared, three of his fellow gang members lay dead in the street along with five members of the rival gangs. Morgan found himself promoted to lieutenant in the gang.

With the new promotion came new responsibilities. Morgan was in charge of selling drugs to the school kids. The other gangs left his fledgling members alone to the relatively small market while they cornered the more lucrative adult market. Morgan and his young gang members flooded the middle schools with drugs.

Morgan and his growing gang graduated to the high school kids after a few overdoses in the middle schools. The high school crowd was more sophisticated in their choices. Morgan had to branch out to different drugs in addition to weed and opioids. The growing Fentanyl craze took him by surprise, but he quickly adapted. When a bad batch took out all the customers in one school, Morgan finally felt the heat of police on his neck.

Two years in juvie gave him a whole new set of skills; it was like going to crime trade school. Running drugs expanded to boosting cars and human trafficking. He learned all the tricks of the trade from the others in detention. The simple refrain from his teachers—"It's the system. It's trying to hold you down. You gotta fight back."

When he got out, he found a new gang and new responsibilities. After he proved himself boosting a couple dozen cars, he was promoted to teach boosting to the newer members. Finally, he was put in charge of them, expanding his influence and gaining new respect among the larger gang's leaders.

Another promotion to lieutenant brought him a bit of notoriety in the local community. Now the gang wanted him running the human trafficking angle. He picked it up fairly quickly, got recruiting and kidnapping down to a science. He was efficient, but could be brutal when the time came for it. He had to beat some of the girls and even some fellow gang members when they got out of hand. Eventually, he got some lieutenants of his own.

Then a rival gang wanted some of their territory and the inevitable war broke out. Up until now, Morgan had only enforced with a bat or a knife, but now he'd been handed a gun.

Morgan was off overseeing a new shipment of runaways at a warehouse outside the city limits when the rival gang hit his gang. The ensuing bloodbath took thirty lives in the next couple of hours between the two factions. When Morgan got back, there was a power vacuum in his organization. Morgan stepped into the role and became the new leader of the gang.

He had to choose his own lieutenants this time. He picked the ones who had been most loyal to him over time. He picked the ones who always had his back. He picked the ones who could bail him out of any trouble. At the top of that list, the man who became his second in command was Jeremy.

Six months of growth, successful recruitment of new gang members, a truce and eventual absorption of the other gang made Morgan a very rich twenty year old man. But with success, comes jealousy.

Morgan looked at Jeremy gasping for breath as he lay in a spreading puddle of his own blood. Morgan knew he should feel exhilaration for defeating a coup, for holding onto his leadership with an animalistic ferocity, but all he felt was shock.

Jeremy had been with him for three years. A friend and ally when sometimes there were none. A betrayal of this level was something Morgan just couldn't compute. They'd had the world, they'd shared every success. They were as close as brothers.

As his friend, former friend, looked up at him with dying eyes, Morgan collapsed into a chair. He looked at the gun again. He'd pulled the trigger. He'd taken a man's life. How did this trouble him when nothing else he had done coming up in the gangs had?

They both had girlfriends. They hung out together. They lived and laughed together. He was going to name his first son after Jeremy. But now this.

The light went out behind Jeremy's eyes and his head slumped to the floor. Morgan cocked his head and looked at his friend. Tears dripped down Morgan's face.

He looked at the gun again. He looked at Jeremy. He stood up and screamed, firing the gun into Jeremy's body again and again, watching it twitch each time.

Morgan fell to his knees and screamed. He shouted at the world until he was hoarse.

Was this what it was going to be like? Always watching everyone, looking out for the next assassin? The friend you drank with the night before would be holding a gun to your head the next day?

"It's the system," Morgan murmured. "It's trying to hold me down... I gotta fight back..."

Morgan looked into the dead eyes of his friend staring back at him. He reached over and pushed Jeremy's eyelids closed. He thought about Jeremy's girlfriend. She'd scream and cry and hate him. He'd have to put her in the business, turning tricks. His own girlfriend would hate him for doing that to Jeremy's girlfriend. Might have to push her out on the street too.

"Ya gotta fight back," Morgan said. "But I don't want to fight back anymore."

Morgan raised the gun to his temple and pulled the trigger.

Moonlight illuminated the fog rolling in on either side of the cargo container as Rudolf opened the padlock and lifted it from the hole in the latch. To his left and right stood his well-armed fellow thugs, Alexei and Dima; they both stepped back and drew their weapons. Rudolf unlatched the door and pulled it up, opening the back of the truck. Rudolf clicked on his flashlight and the women in the back of the truck lifted their hands to block the painful light.

"Out," Rudolf directed the women as he stepped aside and swung his free arm in a sweeping motion toward the interior of the dimly lit warehouse. "*Srochno!*"

The women filed out of the container hurriedly. They were dressed in wildly different outfits. Some were in shorts and t-shirts, others in dresses of various designs, a couple in skirts, and a lucky few in pants, shirts, and jackets, which were some relief against the cold. They shook as much from fear as the temperature. Their hair was messy and disheveled as was to be expected from being stuck traveling for a day in a stuffy cargo container. If they were wearing makeup, it was streaked with mascara from the dried tears on their faces. Rudolf counted the women as they exited. He was about to shut the door when a voice called out from within.

"*Prozhdat'!*"

Rudolf quickly shined the light into the truck and saw a tall woman with black hair perfectly styled in long braids, makeup applied meticulously and dressed in a horse riding outfit—the pants black with the customary riding boots shining like they were freshly polished. Her white blouse was tucked in tight into the pants, accentuating her generous curves. She walked casually past Rudolf, gently swaying her hips so prominently presented in the tight black pants that shined when he passed the flashlight across them.

"Leonid!" Rudolf shouted and there was a shout from around the truck as the driver came to the opening.

"*Da?*" the young man said from the opening.

"You said there were twenty women," Rudolf replied. "I count twenty-one."

"Take it up with Ivan—he counted and loaded them. He told me how many and I drove. I'm going to sleep now," Leonid said and walked away.

"Kretins," Rudolf growled.

"Oh come now, Rudolf," the well dressed woman said from the front of the other women. He noticed how the women crowded next to each another but shied away from the speaker. "You've hired good men who do their job even if their attention to detail is somewhat lacking."

"You," Rudolf said as he squinted his eyes and walked up to her. She was the same height as him and didn't flinch as he approached. "You are *polismen*, eh? Interpol? The truck is shielded and so is this warehouse. Whoever was tracking you has no signal. You're my property now."

"Shielded? Clever," she replied as she smiled. "You know, you're taller than your father Dmitri. Always had a nose for violence, but not much for the business side of things."

"Yes, I like the business side," Rudolf said as he pressed into her and took one of her braids in his hand, feeling it as one would a trader judging the quality of a piece of silk. "You'll fetch a nice price with an oligarch friend of mine in Rublevka. He's been looking for a dungeon wench with big boobs."

"Sounds enticing—I do like chains, just not on me. Tell me, where do you house everyone? Surely not in this big area—do you have cells or perhaps more cargo containers tucked around back?"

"I tire of this conversation, Interpol."

"My name is Antanasia," she interrupted him with a grin.

"I don't care. You can ask questions of your new master in a few hours," Rudolf smiled and stepped back.

"Oh Rudolf, you'll be dead long before my new master is available," she replied and smiled. "But before that, I'll need you to share all that juicy wisdom."

Rudolf swung the hand with the flashlight in it at her face, but she caught his hand with lightning speed and bent it backwards, breaking it at the wrist. Her foot shot out and broke his leg at the kneecap; his leg bent in half the wrong way and he went down. She caught the falling flashlight and swung it down on his shoulder, shattering it with a wet crack as he was falling.

Alexei had just raised his pistol to shoot in her direction when she was at his side grabbing his hand and twisting it around so the trigger pull targeted his open mouth. Blood, bone and brain matter exploded out the back of Alexei's skull.

Before Alexei's body hit the ground, she was behind Dima with Alexei's gun. She fired into the back of both his knees and the elbow of the hand holding his gun. Dima fell to the ground screaming as his gun clattered across the ground to rest by the dead form of Alexei.

She disappeared for a moment and Rudolf tried to crawl toward the opening next to the truck. She reappeared holding Leonid in front of her facing Rudolf. She opened her mouth revealing a row of needlelike fangs. She sank her fangs into Leonid's throat and sucked deeply for several seconds as his eyes rolled up into the back of his head. As Leonid's shaking body went limp, she drew her head back before plunging into his neck again with an animalistic ferocity, tearing at the flesh until his head was severed from his body, soaking her white blouse in red. She casually tossed Leonid's severed head over her shoulder. As blood spurted up from his severed neck, she held the body up so the spurting blood splashed into her mouth, onto her face and in her hair. She shook her head and bathed in the crimson liquid.

When the blood flow slowed to a trickle, Antanasia let Leonid's limp body fall to the floor. She looked at Rudolf and licked her lips. Rudolf's wide eyes got even wider as he skin went from pale to white. She smiled as blood dripped from her jaws down her blouse onto the ground and Leonid's dead body.

"Just a light snack," she said. "Now, Rudolf, about the logistics of this place. I'm looking to expand into food storage, primarily men. They tend to house more blood than women and I don't like to waste storage capacity."

"*Vampir!*" Rudolf squeaked as he clambered away from her on his one good leg and hand. Half of the women fainted, the ordeal from being abducted and traveling a day without food, water or light didn't prepare them to take in the carnage they'd just witnessed. The ones who didn't faint ran for the doors and the opening next to the truck just beyond Alexei's fallen corpse. She paid them no attention.

"Oh Rudolf, was it that obvious? I thought I'd kept my secret identity under wraps so well," Antanasia said as she walked up to him, grabbed his shirt and yanked him up off the floor.

"What gave me away?" she asked, spitting Leonid's fresh blood dripping down her face into her mouth onto Rudolf's shaking, pale visage. Rudolf shamelessly pissed himself as he struggled to escape Antanasia's grasp.

"Please don't kill me!" Rudolf whimpered.

"Aww, you sound just like your dad did," Antanasia purred. "You're already dead, Rudolf, you just don't know it yet. Now, I can make your death slow and painful, or quick and painful. Which would you prefer?"

Rudolf slumped in her grip. "Quick," he said.

"That's a relief," Antanasia replied. "Do you know how hard it is to get a real estate agent to work at night?"

Rudolf groaned.

"So, why don't you house people at this facility long term?"

"Electricity is all by generator, expensive to run all the time. There's no running water. Doesn't work for live product. Facility is abandoned—pay for utilities, draw the eye of the authorities."

Sounds of screams came from outside. Antanasia sighed. "How many guards?"

"Two. Anatoly and Gregor," Rudolf said.

"I'll be right back," she replied. "Don't go anywhere." She dropped Rudolf to the ground and he cried out in pain.

Outside, Antanasia first encountered Anatoly dragging a woman by the hair back toward the warehouse. She simply appeared behind him and twisted his head around, snapping his neck. He fell to the ground and she grabbed the Kalashnikov rifle before it hit the ground. The woman who fell from his grip rolled away and ran off into the night.

Gregor had two women at gunpoint marching in front of him at the opposite end of the road. Antanasia appeared at his side and unleashed the fury of the Russian military rifle on the unsuspecting thug. She continued putting slugs into his dead body until the clip ran out, just to see what damage the weapon would do. Gregor's head was a mass of pulverized flesh, bone and blood. Large bloody, meaty holes dotted his torso.

"That was fun," Antanasia announced to the two shell shocked women standing there. She picked up Gregor's rifle and emptied that clip into his body as well. One of the women ran off screaming and the other simply fainted. Antanasia dropped the spent, smoking weapon on the ground and looked over at the unconscious woman and the one running off in the distance.

"So squeamish," she murmured. "Probably should have a healthier diet."

She returned to the warehouse and walked up to Rudolf. He had crawled halfway across the floor toward the pistol lying next to Alexei's body.

"Rudolf, so naughty," Antanasia said. She picked him up and threw him into the cargo container still sitting open. He hit the far wall off the container with a crack and fell to the floor. She walked up to him again and kneeled down to his face.

"I thought we had a deal?"

Rudolf coughed up some blood and Antanasia shook her head. She lifted his unbroken hand and proceeded to break each finger while reciting the little piggy rhyme.

"There. Now you won't be tempted to go find another gun," she said and propped him up against the wall. "So, do you house the girls in a more residential setting? Perhaps the city? How do you keep them from making noise to alert the authorities?"

"Inner... rooms," Rudolf slurred as a bloody drool streamed from his mouth onto his chest. "Sound... proof...f oam." He coughed again and spit up thick bits of congealed blood and lung tissue.

"No... windows..." Rudolf wheezed out and then his head slumped forward. She picked his head up and could see his eyes still moving, lost in the hazy fog of near death.

"Thank you, Rudolf," she said and then squeezed his head in her hands until it burst. She giggled as the brain matter spurted out through his eye sockets and sprayed all over her blouse.

She stood up and shook herself off. She cracked her neck and stretched. "Well, that was satisfying and illuminating."

Antanasia walked to the edge of the container and transformed into a large black wolf in an instant. She walked around to the lip of the loading dock, jumped off and ran away into the night.

LEGS

Hai Jennings woke up with a headache and groaned. She was face down on soft ground. Her eyes flittered open and in the dark haze, she realized she couldn't identify the ground she was laying on. Was it dirt? The consistency of the earth granules was thick and somewhat silky.

"Ahh, Missus Jennings, it appears you are awake. The process is always a bit random, so it takes a while sometimes," a man's voice echoed around her.

Hai raised her head and saw a gleam on the wall directly in front of her, a reflection of light from somewhere overhead. Beyond the reflection there was nothing but darkness. But in the reflection, she saw herself lying on the ground.

As Hai put her hands down to push herself up, she noticed the shackles on her wrists for the first time, iron manacles attached to chains connected to eyebolts sticking up from the strange ground several feet away from her. She did some quick mental math and realized the eyebolts were effectively out of reach given the lengths of the chains.

"Why am I here?" Hai said as she stood up. She looked up and saw a single man dressed in a dark robe seated at a small desk roughly ten feet up the wall in a small alcove, well out of her reach. He banged a gavel on the desk.

"This intra-psyche court will come to order," the man said. "I am the presiding judge, the honorable Jason Ricketts. You, Hai Jennings, are accused of murder. Eight counts. How do you plead?"

"Innocent. I'm a justice dealer," Hai said and shifted uncomfortably on her feet. The chains were heavy and she let her arms hang to her sides. She looked into the darkness around her and noticed the glare of the light seemed to reflect on the surface of what appeared to be a globe like enclosure. She wondered if the substance was a thick plastic or glass she could somehow break once she could get free of the shackles.

"Your sister is a justice dealer," Jason replied. On the transparent wall to his right a picture of a Chinese woman with an eye patch flashed into existence. She wore black leather with red accents and brandished an energy saber that was red in color. "Ono Quan, quite accomplished even after her sister put out her eye during an altercation ten years ago."

Hai looked at the picture of her sister and scowled. "I don't know this person, but she looks like a liar and a thief," Hai replied. "She could do with a makeover as well. Fairly hideous."

Jason chuckled. "I see she makes quite the impression on your emotions. As to her credentials, they are without flaw and verified by documentation, personal interviews and psychic testing. On the other hand, your credentials, Missus Jennings are, shall we say, questionable under the most extreme scrutiny. You appear to have quite exemplary skills in hacking, forgery and, of course, murder."

"I think you have me confused with someone else," Hai said calmly. She looked at the light on the wall and saw herself standing there in a plain white tunic and khaki pants. Her long black hair was arranged in a tight bun on the crown of her head. She didn't remember changing into this plain and uninspired outfit. Last she could recall she had her hair down.

"You have been placed under a justice province ordered coma to await your trial and sentencing, Missus Jennings. You know this can't be forged or faked. The evidence comes from your own mind for review and judgment by your peers."

"You're hardly my peer, certainly not my equal," Hai said.

Coma? she wondered. She looked down at the eyebolts and tugged on one of the chains. The eyebolt made a brief movement and then the floor around it rippled briefly before becoming solid again. It was all a psychic illusion in her mind. She realized the substance of the clear wall was of little consequence as it didn't actually physically exist. She wondered if the dark chamber was of their design or a reflection of her own psyche's choosing.

"The law says differently, Missus Jennings. As a point of documentation, we are settings the crimes and judgment under your current name, Missus Hai Jennings and not your birth name, Hui-ying Quan or any of the various aliases you have used in the subsequent years since your crimes began."

"Whatever, it's your sideshow," Hai said as she sighed and looked around. She yawned and sat down. There wasn't much else she could do.

"Your latest husband, Alfred Jennings, appears to have succumbed to a unique poison meant to appear like a heart attack," Jason continued. A moving picture from the attacker's point of view showed a balding man sleeping on his side as a syringe was suddenly jabbed into his head behind his ear. A smile almost turned up a corner of Hai's mouth, but she managed to repress it at the last moment. "The standard autopsy revealed no signs of foul play but when we were alerted to your criminal past by Ono Quan, we did a review of the body before cremation and discovered the physical evidence."

"That bitch," Hai murmured. *Should have put out both of her eyes at that fucking reception. Holier than thou show off.*

"Indeed, your sister was tenacious in her pursuit of you in the name of justice," Jason commented. "I can see how that might disappoint one of your proclivities."

"Alfred Jennings was a pedophile and human trafficker," Hai said. "He deserved to die. Punishment was justified."

"Alfred Jennings had no record of any of what you just accused him of," Jason replied. "Of course, since you have dispatched him, we can't search his mind for evidence of any such crimes. There's never even been an accusation on record against him."

"I'm not the only hacker in the world," Hai replied.

"Ah, the conspiracy defense," Jason said and nodded. "Something that could introduce reasonable doubt in the old days, before we could requisition the accused's own thoughts as evidence against them. But if you'd care to recollect any evidence you observed or found of his crimes, you're free to do that now."

On the wall a perfect video came of Alfred sitting at a bench looking at a data tablet. A noise came from the playground twenty feet away and Alfred glanced briefly at the playground before returning his attention to the tablet.

"See, he can't help himself but to look at children," Hai said. "He's a fucking pervert."

"Mister Jennings was an air quality expert looking for possible pollution coming from industrial complexes near neighborhood playgrounds where children congregated," Jason stated. "He glanced up at a sound of possible distress from a child which turned out to just be normal screams of childish delight from a child playing on the equipment. This is the entirety of your evidence?"

"He was a pedophile. I could feel it," Hai said.

"You took the same standard psychic tests for any extra normal abilities as your sister did," Jason said. "You were found to be normal, possessing no special abilities."

"Lies," Hai spat at the ground. "Ono switched the results and stole my place!"

Hai jumped to her feet and ran at the judge but fell flat on her back when she reached the end of the chains. She screamed at the darkness above her.

"Since you never made it beyond the initial screening, you don't know how many tests a justice dealer must pass before they're giving a license to pursue and adjudicate. They are multiple and varied, certainly nothing that can be 'stolen' from someone else."

"Bullshit," Hai said as she crawled back to her original sitting place. "She's no one special."

"But you're special, aren't you Hai?" Jason replied. "That's what you told your eight husbands before you dispatched them."

Unbidden by Hai, each of her previous husbands appeared on the wall and responded with raised eyebrows to Hai telling them she was special. Hai looked down at the floor of the intra-psyche court that had been created in her mind. Her jaws clenched harder with each echo of her telling the men she was special.

"They were all criminals," Hai said. "I was just dealing justice."

"There are no dealings or accusations on record against any of your previous husbands. You criminally hacked databases to change your identity after you received the assets of each of your dead husbands. That alone is proof enough of your avarice and murderous greed," Jason replied. "What remained of those ill-gotten assets has been returned to the surviving members of the victims' families. Your murderous nest egg has disappeared."

Hai jumped to her feet again and raised her hands trying to reach the judge.

"That's my money! They deserved their deaths!"

Jason raised his eyebrows and Hai felt the same venomous hate rise in her throat that she had when her husbands had done the same thing. *He deserves death as well.*

"Let's review the deaths of your husbands, shall we?" Jason asked. "Entered into evidence, the murders of Alfred Jennings, Tyche Brachon, Gregor Fisk, Damone Hasili, Chun Hwui, Victor Lasert, Martin Lyons and Hadris Bartosz."

As each name came up, Hai's point of view popped up on the wall as she dispatched each husband: various poisonings, administration of drug overdoses, a stabbing near an industrial meat grinder, a flare gun at close range knocking a hapless Asian man off a ship at sea and a phone call to an assassin.

"Your response, Missus Jennings?" Jason asked.

"They were pedophiles, abusers, and cutthroats. Every one of them!" Hai shouted.

"Your evidence?" Jason asked. "This is your opportunity to provide for your defense. What in your mind or that you have seen justifies their deaths?"

"I know they did it!" Hai screamed. "They deserved what they got and I deserved their money in recompense!"

"Three of your husbands underwent intense psychological and psychic screening for their classified positions," Jason replied. "All of those things you just accused them of are screened for. Nothing was found. Chun Hwui was screened a week before you killed him. These crimes you think they've committed are all in your mind, unfortunately."

"No," Hai replied in a low hush.

You've suppressed it all just to get me!

"Per the fair judgment protocols, the grand jury watching this adjudication has an opportunity to offer a verdict given the weeks of review of the evidence and witness testimony as well as preliminary evidence presented by your own subconscious last week and today. They have heard from your defense team and are ready to render that verdict."

Up on the wall, the disguised faces of twelve people appeared. Slowly, the words of their verdicts appeared below them. They all read 'guilty.'

"We've identified the particular psychological bend you have. There is no way to treat your particular sickness. Given your subterfuge and hiding of your crimes, this court recognizes you had the capacity to realize what you were doing was a crime. You have been determined to have the mental capacity to determine right from wrong and have chosen to do wrong. You are a danger to your fellow humans. The decisions from the grand jury are unanimous. I'm afraid this court has no choice but to declare you guilty for each crime and to pass judgment."

"Do your worst," Hai said and spat at the ground. "This is all a farce."

"As with all prisoners," Jason continued calmly. "You may end your life as you choose when you feel you can no longer handle your punishment, in accords with the humanitarian requirements of the justice province. Do you understand your rights under this punishment?"

"Go to hell."

"Well, with that statement, I'd say you really do understand. In terms of who may be going to hell, if it exists, I believe you'll have quite the head start on your journey there. First judgment for the first count of murder applied now," Jason said.

Hai's ribs under her right arm cracked and blood stained the tunic as a large insect leg burst forth. It grew out six feet and became segmented. The shiny black tarsal claw at the end of the leg landed on the ground, digging into the dusty black surface. Hai screamed in pain and went to one knee. She looked in horror at the arachnoid limb that had sprung from her body.

"Second judgment for the second count of murder applied now," Jason said. The grisly process repeated out of Hai's left side. She fell to her knees but the two legs seemed to hold up her body somewhat.

Jason repeated the sentence for the third and forth murders as another set of legs sprouted from her body nearer her hips. The ground under her knees was slick with blood. She fell to her hands and knees and the spindly legs adjusted accordingly holding up her entire body weight.

"No!" Hai shouted, blood spitting forth with each word. "They're worthless scum! I was in the right to end them!"

"Fifth judgment for the fifth count of murder applied now," Jason said, his mouth drawn into a grim line and his brow furrowed.

Hai threw her head back and screamed until she was out of breath as the bones in her left arm broke in a million places and reformed as a fifth leg, stretching and ripping her flesh as it transformed. Blood sprayed into the air in a fine mist. The iron manacle fell to the ground, split open by the growing limb.

Hai stumbled in a circle haphazardly on five spider limbs as she was now only tethered to the ground by her left arm. Her human feet drug limply behind her; they were no longer under the control of her mind. Her abdomen swelled into a bulbous black globe as her pants and shirt ripped apart to accommodate the increased surface area. Globs of bloody flesh plopped onto the ground.

"I'll kill you!" Hai screamed. "You're worthless scum like the others!"

"You'll only kill the insects that populate this prison in your mind from here on out," Jason said sternly. "Sixth judgment for the sixth count of murder applied now."

Hai's remaining arm transformed as the first had, the last manacle holding her to the ground broken. She skittered around awkwardly dragging the human limbs behind her. She wasn't quite able to get the hang of walking with the new limbs given the extra baggage at her rear of both the enlarged arachnid abdomen and the fleshy legs that dangled helplessly there.

Her voice was mere guttural growls now as she looked wildly about the ring where she'd been secured. Jason quickly announced the final two judgments and her useless legs were absorbed into the growing abdomen and two more legs sprouted from the rear of the cephalothorax just in front of the abdomen. The last of her clothing fell away revealing an arachnid form with a red hourglass on her abdomen. Her head slowly bubbled and undulated as it transformed into the final piece of the punishment, shrinking back into the cephalothorax sprinting additional eyes that turned black. Two fangs and two pedipalp formed under the eyes to complete the transformation into a black widow. There were no human characteristics left.

The newly formed spider stumbled around the transparent globe that was its temporary home.

"May those who consider taking another's life in anger or in the name of greed heed your punishment and think twice. Under the authority of the justice province, this punishment phase has been broadcast to all citizens. May the gods have mercy on your soul, Hai Jennings."

The walls of the globe disappeared and Jason faded from existence. The human sized black widow skittered away into the dark abyss, hungry and in search of its next meal.

EAR FULL

arv looked out the window at the shrubs moving and looked around to see if there was wind. The fall leaves on the bald cypress trees didn't move at all in the autumn heat.

"Dang varmints," Marv said and spit some tobacco juice into the sink. The brown goo stuck to the side of the metal sink wall and dripped a thin brown liquid down into the drain. He snorted and turned to walk to the gun rack.

He retrieved his shotgun and walked through the living room on his way to the rear sliding door just on the other side of the dining room. His two bluetick coonhounds raised their heads as he passed by.

"Come on," he said to them. "Looks like we got a nasty trash panda or something out back."

The dogs got up and ran to the back door ahead of him. He slid the door open and the dogs ran into the yard.

"Stay!" Marv barked the command and the dogs stopped where they were and looked back at him. They didn't know they were now close enough to trigger the attack from the two dozen raccoons that came streaming out of the brush straight for the dogs.

Marv was so shocked by the sudden emergence of the animals

that he forgot to shout "Come" to get his dogs back inside before the ravenous raccoons overwhelmed his dogs. He shot two of the raccoons off his dogs, but he was too busy reloading before the dogs whimpered their last whimper and stopped moving.

The raccoons all stopped attacking the dogs and looked up at Marv in unison. That was when Marv noticed their eyes had clouded over with a milky substance. He wondered if they could even see him at all. Then the raccoons did the strangest thing he'd ever seen. They nuzzled and rubbed their heads on the fallen canines' heads.

He turned around to go back in the house, but found himself face to muzzle with two black bears. They cocked their heads to the left and then attacked him. Marv never got another shot off before they scratched him with their claws and knocked him into the wall. His head hit the wall with such force, he saw stars and he fell to the ground behind the house. With his head spinning into a tunnel of darkness, he lay bleeding against the step of the porch looking at his decimated pets. He lost consciousness for a while.

When Marv awoke, he saw his two dogs raised their heads. Marv blinked quickly as their milky white eyes looked at him before they got up, walked up to him and nuzzled their heads against him briefly as if saying goodbye. After a brief nuzzle, they joined the raccoons and walked around the building toward the road. Marv lost consciousness again.

Doctor Laura Torres leaned her head back in the chair, her dark brunette hair flowing over the back. The overhead fluorescent lights caught the blue dyed streaks in her hair; her lab partner mused they looked better in direct sunlight.

"It just appears that the worms are consuming the brain matter," Hector Davenport said as he looked again at the slide under the microscope in front of him. "But they didn't start that until much of the internal organs were compromised near to the point of death. It tries to keep the victim alive as it consumes it from the inside."

"Standard parasitic process. I wonder if they're trying to populate by carrion feeders now instead of just birds. But how did they jump species?" Laura asked. "These microscopic parasites don't have a lot of mutation occurring naturally. They've reached their evolutionary end, so to speak. They already have the perfect life cycle."

"These samples were recovered from some raccoons in Louisiana." Hector looked at a map on the wall. He pointed at the coast. "Just south of Baton Rouge near Iberville Parish."

"Iberville? There's a shitload of benzene pollution there. Think it can cause this kind of mutation?" Laura sat up and punched in some searches on her computer and shook her head. "No real limit on the kinds of mutations that can cause. DNA strands are benzene's playground, changing chromosome counts with impunity. Let's dig into the nucleotides and see if we can track the mutations."

"On it," Hector replied. He scratched his ear absently. "Think I might be coming down with a cold. My ear is itchy."

"Drink hot tea and get plenty of rest," Laura said. "You know, you can go home if you're not feeling well. It's not like this research is going to change the world; polluters are going to pollute and there's little we can do to stop that."

Hector looked at the clock. "I supposed I can take off a little early. It's nearly quitting time anyway. I'll grab a quick bite on the way home, brew some tea and call it an early night. Maybe I can head this thing off at the pass."

"Pop some Echinacea and zinc while you're at it. Can't hurt," Laura replied as she got up. "I'll trace the path the mite used to get to the brain in this poor lil trash panda."

"Cool," Hector said as he put the glass slide back in the case and locked it up. "I'll see you tomorrow unless I call in sick."

"Take it easy," Laura said as she put on a pair of gloves and walked back to the dissection room that had the dead raccoon laid out and already open for the autopsy.

Hector walked out the door and Laura closed the door to the inner room. It got deathly quiet as she looked at the inner carcass of one well-dissected raccoon. Where some of the organs would normally be, there should just be a grey goo of partially digested organs. That was the path the typical infestation took at its advanced stages. But if it was too aggressive, the mutated parasites would kill their hosts too quickly and they'd soon die out. At a quick glance, the internal organs seemed unaffected.

She used the forceps to pry the skull back and realized the brain had already been removed and partially dissected on the back counter. She gave the inner skull a cursory examination and noted a strange discoloration near the aural canals. She filed that away in her mind for further analysis later.

She walked around the table and looked at the sections of brain. The discoloration she'd noted inside the skull made a thin path to the center of the brain where it was obvious some of the brain matter had been digested. It had the consistency of glue but should have been spongier.

She took a closer look at the internal organs of the raccoon, but didn't see much in the way of the same infestation of the mites. The organs seemed mostly whole. It showed a difference in diet for this new version of mites.

The raccoon had been exhibiting signs of possible rabies when animal control had trapped it a few days ago. It wandered about in a kind of disorientation that was indicative of either rabies or some sort of brain damage like it had been hit by a car. In this instance, the damage was caused by the mites.

She retrieved the slide Hector had put away and slid it under the microscope. There on the slide, still moving amidst the blood and brain tissue, was a mite much larger than she expected. It appeared to have appendages much larger than normal for that species. As she moved the slide around for a better look, the mite jumped directly at the lens causing her to jump back.

She rubbed her eyes and looked up at the clock. She'd been at it for two hours. Time to go home. She turned and saw Hector standing at the door to the lab. He slowly looked back and forth in the room. Laura was going to call out to him when she noticed his eyes were white and milky.

"What the hell?" she whispered.

Hector staggered into the lab and Laura ducked back behind the door jamb to the dissection room and kept an eye on Hector. He walked into tables and then the walls, not really seeming to realize where he was going or what was in a room he'd worked in for years. He held up his head and sniffed the air. He turned toward Laura, looking right at her and made a kind of gurgling sound as he stumbled forward.

Laura realized she would be trapped in the dissection room if she merely closed the door. She felt her pocket for her cell phone but it wasn't there. She glanced at her desk and saw it sitting there next to the computer keyboard. She darted out into room, staying on the side away from Hector.

She kept her eyes on him and he didn't seem to notice when she moved or respond to any sounds she made, but every time his nostrils flared, he turned in her direction like he was tracking her by scent.

"Hector, are you all right?" she asked as she moved to her desk and grabbed her cell phone. She opened a drawer and pulled out her purse. Hector didn't respond to the sound of her voice. He raised his head and sniffed the air then oriented himself again on where she was in the room. He walked toward her directly, running into the middle of a table. He slowly shuffled his way along the edge until he made it to the end and walked forward again.

"I don't know what's happening to you, Hector, but I'm going to have to lock you in and send... someone to help. I'm sorry," Laura rushed to the laboratory door, walked out and locked the door behind her. She heard a shout to her left and turned to see the director of the laboratory on his knees holding his head. He looked up and screamed and his eyes had turned a milky white.

"Shit," Laura mumbled and ran the other way to the emergency exit. As she exited the building, she noticed half a dozen people outside stumbling along the sidewalk, milky eyes pointed up to the sky, sniffing the air. When her feet hit the sidewalk, they all turned as one and walked toward her.

"Aww hell no," Laura mumbled. She kicked off her heels and ran barefoot to her car. As she got into the car, she glanced around and noticed another dozen people stumbled around the building, all of them sniffing the air. She started the car and drove out of the parking lot.

As she drove away from the lab, she noted the number of people stumbling around lessened. A few people were on their knees holding their heads. Finally, the pedestrians become more normal although a few were running away from the people holding their heads and screaming.

Her mind raced to try to figure out what was going on. Why wasn't she affected like Hector was? Surely they'd both been exposed to whatever was harming Hector and the others. She'd just come back from a field trip to the Amazon and decided the anti-malarial drugs may have contributed to her resistance to whatever was affecting the others. She realized that meant nearly no one in the surrounding town would have the same resistance she did. Whatever this was, it was spreading quickly. She just wasn't sure how.

As she drove out of town, several emergency vehicles raced by her, heading back to where she'd just come from. She didn't stop to find out why they were going back into town. She suspected she knew why and she wasn't sure the emergency personnel would survive the experience. She floored her accelerator and sped away from town.

She made it a few miles outside of town before she had to stop at a roadblock being put up by military personnel. As she came within a few hundred feet of the roadblock, the military personnel raised their weapons and fired at her car. Laura swerved off the road into a tobacco field and got stuck in the moist soil.

Through the shattered windows she was able to hear the military personnel closing in on her. Orders were shouted, but they were followed closely by screams of fear, horror and then agony. Gunfire rang out, but it wasn't directed at her car any longer. Animal growls and screeches accompanied the human sounds of chaos.

Laura frowned. She recognized the animal sounds. It was a puma. No, it was a group of pumas. Laura shook her head. Pumas were solitary creatures, preferring to live and hunt alone. This made no sense.

She got out of the car and made her way back toward the road. As she approached the rise, she lowered herself down and peeked out of the crops growing around her. Several pumas were sniffing around the military men who lay on the ground either dead or incapacitated. The animals sniffed them, rubbed themselves against the men and then wandered off into the undergrowth. One of them looked her way and Laura recognized the white, hazy glazed look in the animal's eyes. She saw the nose sniff for a moment and then turn away, heading into the brush with the other pumas.

They weren't even staying around to eat their kills. It was totally against their instincts and nature, never mind attacking a bunch of armed humans as a group. Laura had to chance it that the surviving military people wouldn't gun her down.

Laura went up onto the road and looked at what she expected to be carnage. The military men were bleeding and disoriented, but it didn't appear any of them were actually dead. She looked off into the crops again, expecting the pumas to return and claim their prize, but the leaves on the tobacco leaves rustled briefly in a light wind and then went motionless. She looked back down at the men on the ground and noticed all of them that were conscious were beginning to scratch at their ears even as they struggled with the pain of the wounds they'd sustained from the animal attack.

Laura gasped as it dawned on her. These wounded would be returned to a medical facility and then may suffer the same as Hector. The pumas weren't exhibiting survival behavior, the mites inside their heads were. This was an intentionally infectiousness organism stretching its new legs.

She looked down the road at the military vehicles sitting idle and ran toward them. One of the men on the ground had enough of his own mind left to reach out to her to stop her, still intent on his original mission. He didn't yet realize he'd become one of those that needed to be stopped; she mused he may never realize that before his own conscious thought ceased and he became a mindless vehicle for the mites. Her mind replayed the videos she'd seen of the half dead insects moving around on their own to attract the attention of their mortal enemies to perpetuate the life cycle of the mites.

She opened the door and saw a soldier hiding on the passenger side of the Humvee. He fired his gun, piercing Laura's throat and spinal column. A jet of blood spurted from her jugular as she fell to the ground.

The soldier screamed and jumped into the driver's seat, putting the car in reverse and running over Laura's legs. She could no longer feel them. As the darkness closed in around her sight, she wondered how humanity would survive.

WINTER OF DISCONNECTION

"Hey sunshine," Lincoln said as he stroked her cheek. "We gotta get out and see the finery in white—it snowed overnight!"

Sherry groaned and stretched under the warm blanket. She blinked her eyes and looked around the unfamiliar room. Her mind clicked and she realized it was the bed and breakfast. The flat screen on the wall of the bedroom was a dead giveaway. Lincoln disappeared into the private bathroom and Sherry flung the covers off and swung her feet over the side of the bed.

She stood up and peeked through the curtains. It looked fresh just like it did yesterday. In fact, it looked exactly the same. Sherry had the strangest sense of déjà vu, but she just shook her head and got dressed. Lincoln walked out of the bathroom and Sherry smiled at him.

"Well," she said. "I'm glad you're in a better mood today than last night."

Lincoln looked at her with a frown. She couldn't be mad at him when she looked into his warm brown eyes.

"I don't think I was in a bad mood," Lincoln replied. "Maybe it was the long drive. I couldn't wait to hit that bed after being on the road so long."

"I guess," Sherry said as she walked into the bathroom. "But you think that would've worn off after a day walking around town."

Lincoln got dressed in silence. Sherry finished getting ready and came out to see Lincoln sitting on the bed staring at her.

"What is it?" Sherry asked. Lincoln pointed at the closet and shrugged.

"You got that new outfit before we left specifically for walking around town the first day. I'm just surprised you aren't wearing it."

"Well, I wore that yesterday," Sherry said as she walked to the closet and looked at the outfit hanging up in the closet with the tags still attached. She looked at Lincoln and frowned.

"Are you sure you're all right?" Lincoln asked. Sherry walked up to him and rubbed his short black curls.

"I'm fine," she said. "I just must be more tired than I thought. Let me change into the new clothes I got and we'll run down to breakfast. Hopefully Darquelle is in a better mood than yesterday."

"I—" Lincoln started and then shook his head. "Never mind. Maybe it's best if you just don't mention yesterday… since we didn't see them yesterday. They got in late after we crashed last night."

Sherry looked at Lincoln and then walked to the closet again. She pulled out the new outfit and nodded her head.

"Right," she said as she tugged at the tags. "My memory must be fuzzy."

When she had changed, they headed downstairs where their friends Henny and Darquelle sat at the big table in the dining room with seating for eight. Darquelle held his head as he pushed scrambled eggs around on a plate.

"Hey, you two," Sherry said. "How are you this morning?"

Henny pressed her hand to her chest and smiled.

"I'm doing fine, but D-man has a headache," Henny said. She playfully rubbed Darquelle's bald head.

"I'm telling you, it's got to be the elevation," Darquelle said.

"What it is is you procrastinating yesterday when we were supposed to leave by two o'clock and you kept your face in the computer working until eight," Henny sat down next to her husband and picked up her fork. "You made the day longer than it had to be and that's why you have a headache today. You're tired and grouchy, like I knew you would be."

"Oh, just like yest—" Sherry began, but then stopped as Lincoln walked in and shook his head. He placed their plates down on the table. "Uh, I mean, have you taken anything for it?"

"He's had some meds already," Henny said. "He'll be fine in an hour."

"Great," Sherry replied and ate some of the eggs.

"Well," Henny continued. "He'll still be grouchy until he crashes for a nap at two like he always does first day of vacation."

"I don't always do that," Darquelle protested.

"No," Lincoln replied. "Just the last ten Christmases we've spent with you."

"You," Darquelle said, pointing his fork at Lincoln. "Are supposed to be my ally. These ladies don't need any help busting my balls, thank you very much."

Everybody laughed and they finished their breakfast in relative silence.

The main street in Leavenworth was just as festive as advertised. The friends enjoyed the shopping and decorations until, as predicted, Darquelle had to take a break for a quick nap around two o'clock.

"I'll take Grumpus back to the BnB," Henny said as she grabbed Darquelle's arm. "You two enjoy. We'll catch you for dinner?"

"Sounds great," Lincoln said.

"Hey," Henny shouted as she walked away. "I heard there are some great vintage shops around—I know how you love that old stuff."

"Thanks!" Sherry shouted and grabbed Lincoln's arm. "Come on—let's go find some hippie shit!"

As they turned, Lincoln pointed at a man with grey curly hair walking toward them.

"Well. I'll be—" Lincoln started but Sherry stepped forward.

"Hi there, it's Edward, isn't it?" Sherry asked.

The man looked up at her in shock. Lincoln also frowned.

"How do you know Edward?" Lincoln asked.

"Oh, well I…uh, I'm not quite sure," Sherry frowned. "But you two worked together at the Institute, right?"

Lincoln nodded but kept frowning. "He left before I met you," Lincoln said. "I don't remember talking about him."

"Interesting," Edward said. "You remember…"

"Well, of course I remember," Sherry said. "You were here because of your wife, I think. The details are a little fuzzy."

"She died," Edward said. "I came here in a misguided attempt to recapture the magic she felt here. I didn't fully realize…"

Edward trailed off and seemed to try to remember something.

"I'm sorry, I didn't realize she'd passed," Lincoln said.

"It was a week ago," Sherry murmured.

"Exactly right," Edward said and gave Sherry his full attention. "But I told you that yesterday and then you died, so that must be why you remember!"

"What?" Lincoln said. "She didn't die. She's right here."

Edward waved him off.

"You didn't die, so you won't remember anything from the last loop."

"Last loop?" Lincoln said. "I can see not much has changed since the Institute; you're still talking in riddles and circles."

"I'm not dead," Sherry chided Edward. "Maybe you've been working too hard... since your wife's death... last week."

Sherry frowned.

"Not hard enough," Edward replied. "I didn't take all the factors into account and now I've got this mess. Of course, you won't really understand, but maybe you can help."

Edward looked into Sherry's eyes. "You died from an allergic reaction to dinner. Not sure what exactly," Edward said.

"That's damn creepy, Edward, even for you," Lincoln objected.

"My apologies, Lincoln," Edward bowed his head. He looked at Sherry again. "Look for the dark eyed ones. That should convince you. I'll see you again."

Edward walked around them and disappeared around a corner. They watched him go with mouths wide open.

"That's the damnedest thing," Lincoln said and shook his head.

"Yeah," Sherry said. "Let's just forget it and go check out that vintage shop. Cool?"

Lincoln gave a half smile and nodded. They joined arms and walked down the sidewalk.

An hour later, Sherry posed in a shop with a floppy hat. She made duck lips at Lincoln and he laughed. As she twirled around, she caught the shopkeeper staring at her with a vacant stare, her eyes completely black. She stopped twirling and looked back at the shopkeeper, but the woman had gone back to folding shirts.

"What is it?" Lincoln asked, looking at the shopkeeper as well.

"Nothing," Sherry whispered and then laughed. "Maybe I should pay attention to my hydration. Let's go find some hot chocolate, okay?"

"Sure thing," Lincoln said.

Sherry put the hat back on the rack and took one more look at the shopkeeper, who looked at her and smiled; her eyes were completely normal. Sherry smiled back and turned to Lincoln.

"Let's go," she said and they walked out of the shop back onto the white dusted sidewalk. A cool wind rushed up the street and sent a flurry of snow up into the air. Sherry shivered. Lincoln pulled her across the street after he looked for traffic. He tugged her into a little coffee shop. They walked up to the counter and ordered two hot chocolates.

They sat down at a small table next to the window and looked out at the other shoppers walking by. Some of the groups had children, who laughed and played, picking up the snow and making impromptu snowballs to throw at each other.

"I'm going to run to the restroom real quick," Lincoln said. Sherry nodded at him and looked back out the window. A few moments passed and she felt someone brush up against her. She looked over and the barista was standing uncomfortably close. Sherry looked up and saw the same black eyed stare she'd seen from the shopkeeper across the street. She gasped.

"You'll be joining us soon," the barista said and then turned away. She walked back behind the counter and resumed cleaning. When she looked back up as a customer entered, her eyes had returned to normal. Sherry just stared at the barista until Lincoln passed back by her on the way to take his seat.

"Everything all right?" Lincoln asked.

"What exactly did Edward do at the Institute?" Sherry asked as she continued staring at the barista.

"Well, he was a theoretical physicist. We got a lot of grants to look into theories on other dimensions, teleportation and the effects of gravity on space travel. A bunch of basically theoretical stuff," Lincoln sipped his hot chocolate and looked out the window.

"What about opening portals between dimensions?" Sherry asked. The barista finished with the customer. As the customer walked away, the barista again looked at Sherry with the same black eyes and grinned.

"Well, I couldn't really say," Lincoln replied.

"Because it's classified," Sherry asked. She turned to look at Lincoln who continued to look out the window.

"Because I couldn't say," Lincoln said. "The work at the Institute was highly compartmentalized, classified yes, but there was really no way to know what someone else was working on unless you worked directly with them. I never worked with Edward. We met at department meetings and the occasional professional conference, but our fields of expertise never crossed paths in the scientific world."

He turned to look at her. He put his hand on top of hers.

"Molecular biology is nowhere near as sexy as theoretical physics. I don't know what you ever saw in me," Lincoln smirked and Sherry smiled grimly back at him.

"Molecular biology is very important in cooking," Sherry replied.

Lincoln nodded. "My secret weapon to your heart through your stomach."

Sherry looked back at the barista who was now helping another customer, her eyes returned to normal.

"Let's go check on our friends," Sherry said. "Surely, Darquelle is rested up by now."

"Okay," Lincoln replied. They got up and left the warmth of the coffee shop and were back in the windy street pushing their collars up.

When they walked into the BnB, Henny looked up from the book she was reading in the living room. She cocked her head at them and her black curls flopped over her face a bit.

"He's still sacked out," Henny said. "Or did you come back for a little afternoon delight?"

"Afternoon what?" Lincoln asked.

"Never mind," Henny said. "You don't have the grasp of musical history I do to appreciate it."

"Well, I do feel like freshening up a bit," Lincoln says. "Got a song for that?"

"Fresh by Kool and the Gang?" Henny said. Lincoln shook his head. "You've got no culture, like at all."

Lincoln shrugged his shoulders and went upstairs.

Sherry sat down on the couch next to Henny and looked back to where Lincoln had disappeared. She turned back to Henny.

"I think I've got a problem," Sherry said.

"He may not know music, but he's a catch otherwise," Henny smirked.

"He's fine," Sherry said. "But there's something weird going on in town."

"Is this because you're a mixed couple?" Henny asked. "I thought you guys had moved past that? Some people are just gonna stare. They're just jealous. You know that."

"Henny, I'm serious," Sherry looked back again to ensure Lincoln was still upstairs.

"All right, girl. Spill."

"We ran into an old co-worker of Lincoln's and he told me I died last night," Sherry looked at Henny with a frown.

"Did you guys go into town last night and do karaoke before you crashed here?" Henny giggled. "You know I can't sing, but I can pick out the best songs for everyone so they don't kill the room."

"Henny, I'm serious," Sherry leaned back on the couch and covered her eyes with her hands. "And I've been seeing people with black eyes—solid black eyes—all day. I can't make heads or tails of any of it."

Henny patted Sherry on the leg reassuringly. "Honey, you're definitely in the right place—you need a vacation!"

Sherry groaned.

Lincoln came back downstairs and sat down in the chair next to Sherry. "Okay, ladies, I've got the evening planned. We're going to start out with a little wine tasting and buying at Baroness Cellars, then we'll take a little walk down to Visconti's for dinner and, of course, more wine."

"Sounds great," Sherry said with a thin smile.

"I do love me some wine," Henny said. "I can hear Darquelle going on about the bouquet or some such nonsense now."

"It's not nonsense!" Darquelle shouted as he entered the room.

"Well, I'm sure you'll tell us all about it," Henny said with a grin. Darquelle walked over to her and gave her a quick kiss.

"You're darn right I will," Darquelle said. "Now let's get this show on the road. The wine ain't gonna drink itself, but someone might beat us to it."

They all laughed and for a brief moment Sherry felt the darkness she'd felt for the last two hours lift a little.

The wine tasting went over well with Darquelle's observations leaving the foursome in stitches. As the sun disappeared over the horizon, they made the short trek two blocks away to Visconti's and got their reserved table quickly.

As Sherry looked over the menu, she started to tune out the others at the table. She looked over the items and wondered which one would kill her. She didn't remember having a food allergy. Was there something in one of these foods or perhaps something was contaminated with something. When the waiter finally arrived, everyone made their order and Sherry looked up from the menu with a frown on her face.

"Miss, your order? Do you need more time?" The waiter said. He looked to be in his mid-twenties. Sherry mused he was probably just making his way through college, the same way she did waiting tables not too long ago. Sherry shook her head.

"You know, I've just kind of lost my appetite. I think I'm going to skip ordering anything," she said with a wan smile. Everyone looked at Sherry with wide eyes, except for the waiter's eyes, which had just turned solid black.

"You can't avoid fate," the waiter said darkly. Then the darkness faded from his eyes and they returned to normal.

"Fate," Lincoln chuckled. "Dude, it's just dinner."

"What?" the waiter said. "Fate? I just asked if she'd like more time. Do you need more time?"

"Just water please," Sherry said and looked down at the table.

"Okay, well if you change your mind, my name is Ken and I'll be happy to take care of you. I'll just get everyone's order in and be back with drinks shortly," Ken said and walked away. Lincoln and Darquelle raised their wine glasses and toasted the beautiful evening and friends. They all raised their glasses and toasted. Sherry looked at Henny who watched her with sad eyes. Henny patted her hand on the table.

"Maybe don't drink the water he brings to the table," Henny said smiling. "Just sayin.'"

Sherry gave her a half smile and noticed someone behind Henny looking at them from another table with the same black eyes the waiter had. They locked eyes with Sherry and then slowly turned back around to the others at their own table.

Dinner was uneventful after that, but Sherry didn't feel like staying out late to party that night, so they all headed back to the

BnB. That's when they found Edward sitting on the steps waiting for them.

"Edward," Lincoln said. "I'm a little surprised to see you here. Do you need something?"

Edward nodded and looked at Sherry.

"You changed the outcome tonight, so I'm hopeful we can work together to break the cycle. I'll talk with you again tomorrow…well, in the morning," Edward said. "Good night everyone."

Edward walked away and Lincoln laughed. "He's so damn eccentric," Lincoln said. Sherry didn't say anything but continued to watch Edward walk away until he was out of sight.

"Sleep is going to be welcome," Sherry said. "I'm just not so sure about waking."

They all walked into the BnB and said their good nights before retiring for the night.

"Hey sunshine," Lincoln said as he stroked her cheek. "We gotta get out and see the finery in white—it snowed overnight!"

Sherry groaned and stretched under the warm blanket. She blinked her eyes and looked around the room. She realized immediately she was in the bed and breakfast. Lincoln disappeared into the private bathroom and Sherry flung the covers off. She looked down at her pajamas and realized they were the same ones she'd woken up in the previous morning, but not the ones she put on last night. She swung her feet over the side of the bed and sat up.

"This is crazy," she whispered. She stood up and walked to the curtains. She reached to pull them open to look outside, but hesitated. She looked back at the bathroom and heard Lincoln shaving with his electric razor.

She peeked through the curtains. It looked fresh, identical to when she looked before. She walked to the closet and pulled out the outfit she'd worn before. It still had the tags on it that she had removed before. Lincoln walked out of the bathroom and Sherry smiled at him.

"Oh, I really like that new outfit you got," Lincoln said. "Can't wait to see you in it."

He gave her a quick kiss and went back in the bathroom.

When she had changed, they headed downstairs where their friends Henny and Darquelle sat at the big table in the dining room as they had before. Darquelle held his head as he pushed scrambled eggs around on a plate.

"Hey, you two," Sherry said. "How are you this morning?"

Henny pressed her hand to her chest and smiled.

"I'm doing fine, but D-man has a headache," Henny said. She playfully rubbed Darquelle's bald head.

"I'm telling you, it's got to be the elevation," Darquelle said.

"What it is is you procrastinating yesterday when we were supposed to leave by two o'clock and you kept your face in the computer working until eight." Henny sat down next to her husband and picked up her fork. "You made the day longer than it had to be and that's why you have a headache today. You're tired and grouchy, like I knew you would be."

"You'll be good as new after a nap," Sherry said almost in a daze. The day on repeat was distracting her.

Lincoln appeared with plates for both of them, but before they could sit down, there was a knock at the door. Lincoln went to the door and opened it. Edward smiled at him.

"Lincoln! So nice to see you again. Can I have a word with your lovely wife, Sherry?" Edward said as he rubbed his hands together to warm them.

"Umm, sure, Edward," Lincoln said as he stepped back and held the door open. "Why don't you come in out of the cold?"

"Thank you," Edward replied and stepped inside the house. Lincoln closed the door and directed Edward to the couch in the living room.

"I didn't know you knew my wife," Lincoln said.

"Just recently met her, actually," Edward replied. "Funny story I'll have to tell you about some time."

"Funny, mmm hmm," Lincoln said. Sherry appeared at the entry to the living room.

"Edward," Sherry said. "This is unexpected."

"Well, the day continues forward regardless what we do to try to change things," Edward said.

"You trying to stop time?" Lincoln chuckled.

"Could we have a moment in private?" Edward asked.

Lincoln frowned and looked at Sherry. She just shrugged.

"Sure," Lincoln said. "Don't want my breakfast to get cold."

He raised his eyebrows at Sherry. She smiled at him grimly and walked into the living room to sit next to Edward. Lincoln took one last look at them and then shook his head. He walked into the dining room.

"I apologize for the intrusion, but I needed to workshop a solution to our dilemma," Edward whispered.

"Lincoln is going to suspect something unseemly if we carry on like this," Sherry whispered back. "I don't need him thinking anything like that!"

"Well he won't remember any of this anyway, so you should be fine," Edward said. "Unless he somehow dies, then he'd be in on the loop as well, but I don't recommend it."

"Dies? Look, I'm still here. I didn't die last night like you said," Sherry said. "But, there was some weird things going on."

"The dark eyed beings visited, yes?" Edward said knowingly.

"It was normal people and then their eyes," Sherry shuddered.

"I think they're from the other side, temporarily inhabiting people," Edward said.

"The other side of what?"

"I wasn't entirely truthful yester… uh, day," Edward frowned. "Hard to keep track of time. Anyway, I didn't come here to capture the magic of my wife; I came here to bring her back."

"To life? Like Frankenstein?" Sherry frowned.

"No, not like that. I… built a portal to pierce the veil between life and death and… well, I think I was successful, but it clearly didn't turn out like I thought it would."

Sherry sat there with her jaw agape.

"How did you *think* that was going to turn out?" Sherry hissed.

"Well," Edward looked around uncomfortably. "I thought I would walk her back across the veil. I thought it was a recent enough death that her spirit might still be lingering here and… I was wrong."

"Yeah, undoing death is a little more complicated than building a door," Sherry scoffed. Edward frowned.

"I built a device that attenuated the frequencies between the realms of life and death creating a stable portal. It's a bit more complicated than simply building a door."

"So shut the door, portal or whatever you call it," Sherry said.

"That's a bit of a problem," Edward grinned awkwardly. "Like you, I've crossed the veil even if briefly and now I live in both worlds, much like you. We're not affected by the same laws of time and space, but it also means, for some reason, I can't physically affect the machinery. I suspect you will be similarly afflicted."

"Suspect? You mean you don't know," Sherry stood up.

"It's a working hypothesis—what do you want from me, I've never done this before." Edward stood up as well.

"Never done what before?" Lincoln said as he walked in.

"Genius here pierced the veil, now we're both living in two dimensions at once and we can't shut down the portal," Sherry said. She looked at Edward. "That sound about right?"

"Not exactly how I would've phrased it, but yes," Edward said as he scowled at her.

"Is this a sex thing?" Lincoln frowned as he said it.

"*No!*" they both shouted in unison.

"It's a dead thing," Sherry said. "I died. Crossed right over that veil and now I'm stuck here."

"Your death was not my fault," Edward said.

"I bet you say that to all the girls," Sherry retorted and then gasped. "Oh, I'm sorry Edward."

Edward looked down and walked to the door.

"I won't have the luxury of forgetting this, unfortunately," Edward said as he opened the door and shut it behind him.

Lincoln looked at Sherry, then at the door, and then back at Sherry.

"That was awkward and I'm not even sure what happened," he said.

"He's right," Sherry said as she sighed. "You're not going to remember anything. This sucks."

Sherry walked around the couch heading for the dining room.

"Oh, but I will," Lincoln said as he turned to Sherry, his eyes now solid black. He leaped over the couch and collapsed on top of Sherry driving her to the ground. She struggled with him as he tried to choke the life out of her. "Let's find out what happens when you die again!"

With a clatter of dishes, Henny and Darquelle abandoned their breakfast and rushed to pull Lincoln off of Sherry.

"Lincoln, stop it!" Henny shouted. As they grabbed him, he looked at both of them with pure black eyes and laughed.

"You'll all join us soon!" Lincoln cackled and then went limp.

Sherry scrambled away from them and jumped to her feet.

"Don't hurt him! He's not himself!" Sherry shouted.

Darquelle and Henny looked at Sherry in shock as they held Lincoln's limp body up.

Lincoln stirred and blinked his eyes. They had returned to normal.

"What's going on? Did I faint? Did I have a stroke?" Lincoln asked. He stood on his own and they released their grip on him.

"This stops today," Sherry announced.

"You're not going to divorce him," Henny pleaded. "Try counseling first!"

"Henny, I've always been skeptical of your hocus pocus nonsense, well I'm not anymore. The dead are trying to take over this world. We have to stop them from getting a foothold," Sherry said as she walked to the front door.

"Well, what if I want to be skeptical?" Henny said as she looked at Darquelle and Lincoln, who was still trying to shake off the effects of his brief possession.

"Eh, brother has glossy black olives for eyeballs, you can't be skeptical anymore," Darquelle said.

"We need to find—" Sherry started as she opened the door and saw Edward standing there. "Edward!"

Sherry hugged him and he looked bewildered.

"Uh, I'm glad to see you too," he replied.

"Grab your jackets," Sherry said as she ran back in to the closet by the stairs. "We're going to see that portal of yours, Edward."

Edward pulled the SUV up to park behind his own sedan by the side of the road. To the left of the car, a road was washed out. It was still traversable by foot or a four wheel drive vehicle operated by a skilled driver. The crew in the car was anything but skilled at four wheeling.

Edward and his fellow scientist, Lincoln, had great scientific skills, but weren't too outdoorsy. Sherry was a great financial manager and businesswoman in her own right, but that didn't extend to success in the back country. Henny ran her own physical rehabilitation clinic and worked alongside her partner of ten years, Darquelle; they met at college and she'd graduated one GPA point ahead of him and never let him live it down in their more teasing moments. They were perhaps the most physically adept of the group, but that covered hiking and skiing, not off road vehicle expertise.

Up the hill sat an abandoned house sitting next to a landslide. The area had been deemed too geologically unstable to remain inhabited and its remote location made it undesirable to most squatters. That made it an excellent location for a space/time experiment.

"Shouldn't we have weapons?" Lincoln asked as they climbed out of the car.

"That would just make those under temporary possession that much more dangerous to the others and themselves," Edward said. "My tools in the house may be of some concern from that standpoint."

"Fantastic," Lincoln replied. "I'm both reassured and overtly concerned. Thanks Edward."

Sherry smiled as they climbed down into the small gulley and then back up the other side.

"You carted everything over there yourself?" Sherry asked.

"Well," Edward replied. "I used physical elements from the structure itself to stabilize the portal. I mostly just added some calibrating equipment and vibration generators to it."

"Sounds easy to dismantle," Darquelle said as he helped Henny over a log on their way up the hill.

"It was meant to be temporary," Edward said. "It wasn't until I briefly crossed over that I found I couldn't affect the portal or the elements that were stabilizing it."

"Crossed over?" Henny said. "You mean you died?"

"Well," Edward said. "It's complicated."

"No kidding?" Lincoln said. "You created a portal that pokes a hole in our dimension; you'd think it was as simple as stubbing your toe on a wormhole in space."

"How long were you over there, Edward?" Henny asked as they topped the hill and stood in front of a two story log cabin with a collapsed side building half buried under the landslide.

"Umm," Edward said. "It's hard to say. I'm not entirely sure time passes the same in both dimensions. It felt like an eternity, but I returned to exactly the same point in time when I crossed back over with the obvious unforeseen complication of being stuck in a temporal loop. I immediately tried to shut down the portal, but it resists my attempts to interfere."

"Resists your attempts?" Darquelle asked.

"Let's go inside and I'll show you. The portal is at the doorway between the living room and the kitchen," Edward said as he walked forward. "Hope you ate well. I can't offer any food at this time since the kitchen's in a different dimension."

"I gotta use that excuse next time we host a party," Darquelle said. Henny punched his arm lightly.

They followed Edward through the front door into a large living room that looked like it had been stripped of all valuables, leaving behind just the heavy furniture that would have been very difficult to get across the chasm leading to the house. Even the cushions on the large wooden couch had been removed.

"Sturdy, but not very inviting," Lincoln quipped.

Edward pointed forward to a doorway that was simply the darkest black anyone could remember seeing. The edges shimmered with a silvery, pulsating border that looked like living metal.

"I love what you've done with the place," Darquelle said.

"Honestly, Darquelle," Henny chided.

Sherry stepped forward and touched the metal boxes attached to the wall around the portal.

"Looks like I can touch them after all," Sherry said.

"Interesting," Edward remarked. He pointed to the empty spot in the living room. "I'll show you what happens when I try, but I recommend you step well out of the way. The knockback is a bit unpredictable."

"Knockback?" Lincoln asked.

"It knocked me out briefly yesterday," Edward replied. "I'm not really keen to experience it again, but the data could be valuable."

"Always the scientist," Lincoln murmured and stepped away into the interior of the living room.

Edward observed his companions to make sure they were far enough back and then reached toward the box closest to them. There was a spark and hum as Edward was thrown back several feet landing on his back.

Everyone but Lincoln ran to check on Edward. Lincoln cocked his head and looked at the portal and the wheels in his head were turning.

"It's the resonance," Lincoln said.

The others helped Edward to his feet. He brushed off some of the dirt and sniffed.

"I smell a bit of burnt flesh," Edward replied. "It's a bit more than resonance."

"No," Lincoln said. "I mean you were on the other side so long, you may have changed the resonance of your own atomic structure, putting you more far side than this side."

"That's a disappointing hypothesis," Edward replied. "That portal being active may be the only thing allowing me to survive on this side.”

Lincoln frowned and looked at Sherry. “Wait, what do you mean it looks like you can touch it?” Lincoln asked.

“Well, I died two days ago, two loops ago? I’m not sure anymore,” Sherry said.

“Died?” Lincoln asked. “I don’t think so, I’ve been with you every... moment.”

Lincoln felt faint and caught himself on the couch.

“If we shut this thing down...” Lincoln held his head. “What happens to Sherry?”

“Hypothetically, she’s more of this dimension than the other,” Edward said. “Perhaps that means she’s more anchored here and will survive.”

“But she died,” Lincoln said and stepped forward to Edward. “She could just revert to being dead.”

“Lincoln, I just don’t know,” Edward said. “It’s all hypothetical. We’re dealing with realities we’ve never experienced before.”

“I could be on borrowed time,” Sherry said. “But if anyone else dies in this loop, then the same thing could happen to them. We have to shut this thing down, Lincoln.”

“Do we?” Lincoln asked. He stepped over to Sherry and held her hands. “We could just experience the same day over and over together forever. Would that be so bad?”

“This may not be forever, Lincoln,” Sherry said. “We don’t know what the dark ones want. This might just be a stepping stone to them. What if this spreads across the world and we’re all trapped in a loop of encroaching darkness. Maybe it will only last until they’re powerful enough to make it permanent and then they start time again and everybody dies.”

“I love you,” Lincoln said taking her face in his hands. “I don’t want to lose you.”

Sherry put her hands on his. "If you love me, we'll find each other across the dimensions. Nothing can keep us apart," she said and smiled. He kissed her and they held each other.

"I don't mean to break up this wonderful moment," Henny said gently. "But I thought there was going to be some resistance from dark eyed dudes when we tried to shut this down."

"They watched me get repelled a few times after they tried to dissuade me from touching the machinery and then their numbers dwindled. There's usually a watcher somewhere, but I haven't seen any," Edward said.

"But they knew we were coming," Sherry said.

"Maybe they're not concerned about us shutting it down anymore. Are we too late?" Darquelle asked.

"No!" Edward shouted. "It can't be! We can't let this stand. I can't..." Edward reached for the wall to hold himself up. "I just wanted to find her."

"What if that isn't the dimension of death," Sherry said. "What if she was never there to begin with, Edward? You'll find her where she really is—on the other side, but that isn't the other side where she's at."

Sherry pointed at the portal.

"I did the measurements," Edward said. "Do you think my calculations were off?"

"A lot of this has been off," Lincoln said. "You said it yourself. This wasn't what you meant it to be."

"I suppose," Edward said. "In any case, we need to shut it down."

Edward walked to the portal and pointed carefully at the two bread box sized enclosures mounted to the wall on either side of the portal.

"If you strike these simultaneously, it should reduce the

shockwave when the portal closes."

"Shockwave?" Darquelle asked. "Like that thing that knocked you back?"

"Something like that," Edward answered. "I mean, it's all hypothetical, but I did design shutdown buffers into the devices."

"Maybe Sherry and I should do the honors," Lincoln said. "If something happens to both of us, then—"

"Nope," Henny said. "You two couldn't swing anything simultaneously. Darquelle and I are in the gym all the time. We got this. You two hold each other in case, well, you know…"

Henny grabbed Darquelle who briefly protested but went along with Henny to the portal. Edward handed them both hammers.

"Just strike them on the top and they should fall off and fall out of sync, closing the portal."

Darquelle groaned and Henny cleared her throat. He sighed and stood up straight, hammer at the ready. Henny raised hers as well.

"Bring it down on three. One, two, three!" Henny said and they both swung the hammers down. The boxes sparked as they fell off the wall. Henny and Darquelle jumped back to avoid the falling boxes. A low frequency hum that had been in the background suddenly ceased. The edges of the portal shimmered briefly, but then went back to normal. The portal remained open.

"Well, shit," Darquelle said.

"I don't understand," Edward said as he stared at the portal.

"It can't be permanent, can it?" Lincoln asked.

Edward shook his head.

"No, it's not possible to keep a stable portal between the dimensions without some mechanism," Edward said and then snapped his fingers. "They stabilized it on the other side. Now it makes sense why they weren't worried about us destroying this side."

"What do we do?" Darquelle asked.

"No," Edward said as he picked up a hammer. "It's what do I do? I'm already attuned to the other side. It only makes sense I cross over again and destroy the portal once and for all."

Lincoln stepped forward and grabbed his arm to stop him as he walked toward the portal.

"Edward, you may not survive this," he said. "I'm sorry this happened, but thank you for doing what you can to fix it."

Edward smiled grimly and nodded at him. "You may want to clear the premises," Edward said. "I really have no idea what might happen."

They left quickly, but Lincoln jammed a big rock in the door to keep it open. They wanted to see what happened if they could. They gathered a few yards from the front door and watched Edward look at them, wave and then enter the black portal, disappearing from view.

After a few minutes, the portal shimmered briefly and then the door way returned to normal, light streaming in through the kitchen windows.

"Edward?" Sherry shouted out. She looked down at her hands and saw nothing had changed. "I'm still here," Sherry said. "It must have worked, but I didn't disappear."

"Edward?" Lincoln shouted as he walked toward the building. The building shook and the porch cracked.

"Let's not wait for the thing to collapse," Darquelle said. "It worked, portal's down. I think we all knew Edward was probably not coming back through, didn't we?"

Henny turned away from the damaged house and shook her head.

"I didn't know him long, but that seemed a harsh fate," Henny said. "I need a drink."

"I think we all do," Lincoln replied. He grabbed Sherry's hand but she resisted and kept looking at the building. "Honey, what is it?"

"This isn't done," Sherry said. "I can feel it."

"We shut down Edward's crazy portal," Lincoln said. "I think that's enough for today, don't you?"

"Yeah, I guess so," Sherry replied and turned to him with a grim smile. "A loss and a win. Bittersweet."

They made their way down the hill and back up the gulley. As they climbed into their car, Sherry shed a tear.

When they got back to downtown Leavenworth, one of the wineries had just opened and they walked in to get a good helping of wine to toast Edward's memory. The day progressed normally. Sherry saw no more people with black eyes staring her down. She still skipped dinner, just to be sure.

The next morning, she stretched as Lincoln climbed on the bed.

"Hey sunshine," Lincoln said as he stroked her cheek. "We gotta get out and see the finery in white—it snowed overnight!"

The color drained from her face as Sherry slowly got out of the bed and went to the closet. Her outfit for the first day on vacation still had the tags on it. She ripped them off in frustration, tearing the blouse sleeve. She ran to the window and looked out at a familiar sight. The new fallen snow looked exactly the same as it had before.

"Poor Edward," she said. Lincoln came up behind her and chuckled. It was a dark, gurgling sound unlike any she'd heard before. She turned slowly to look at him and he stared back at her with pure black eyes.

"Did you really think we didn't have a backup plan?" Lincoln asked before he wrapped his hands around her throat.

ANALYSIS

Greg walked into the office and checked his blonde hair in the mirror hung up just inside the door. An audible buzz from inside the office alerted the personnel inside that someone had arrived. Just below the mirror was a plaque that read "It's okay to ask for help." Behind him, Adriana stood with her arms folded.

"It's not even your hair," she said. "Is your vanity so strong that you can't pass a mirror without checking out the skin you're in?"

Greg snorted and smiled at her. He stepped all the way into the office so Adriana could as well. She gave the mirror a quick glance as she passed it just to check her own hair and makeup. She raised her eyebrows—the lipstick shade wouldn't have been her first choice, but it seemed to go well with her complexion. Eyebrows could use a little darkening. She wondered if the light eyebrows were a symptom of premature aging. She shook her head, realizing it didn't really matter.

She stopped next to Greg and they both looked at the receptionist sitting behind a small oak desk. The receptionist, an older woman with auburn hair graying in streaks, looked up at them and smiled.

They looked to the left and saw a single young man sitting there nervously rubbing his hands together. He looked up at the two of them and they noted his striking blue eyes matched his ginger curls so perfectly. Adriana smiled at the young man. The young man's mouth curled up slightly at the recognition and then fell as the young man looked down and returned to his fidgeting.

The receptionist remained seated.

"Can I help you?" she asked.

Greg rubbed his fledgling beard and pondered for a moment. "Yeah, a little anyway," he replied. The two of them walked up to the desk. Adriana folded her arms and smiled, cocking her head to the right causing her jet black hair to ripple as it settled.

"Remember when they stood up whenever you entered a room? I miss those days," Adriana whispered. Greg grunted in agreement.

"What do you need?" the receptionist asked as she opened up a manual calendar and picked up a mechanical pencil. She clicked it once and then looked back up at them.

"We need a joint appointment," Greg replied.

"Okay," the woman said as she flipped through the calendar and stopped after two pages. "Doctor Furnstein's first available appointment is in two weeks on the twenty-seventh. There will be double the charge for two patients, of course."

Greg looked at Adriana and she shook her head. "You see," Greg said. "The thing is we have a lot of things planned over the next couple of days that will keep us from making an appointment in two weeks. Any chance he could squeeze us in today?"

"Doctor Furnstein is in high demand," the receptionist replied with a smile. "Since his appearance on Doctor Hank's show, he's had any amazing uptick in business. That appointment in two weeks is probably the only one for the next couple of months."

Greg looked at Adriana again and she nodded toward the receptionist. Greg sighed and turned back to the woman holding the pencil at the ready. "I mean, this is a matter of life and death," Greg said. "Are you sure you can't help us out here?"

"There's really nothing I can do," she replied as she set the pencil down. "But I can refer you to the public mental health clinic, if you like. They might be able to see you this week."

Greg turned to Adriana. "See, I'm no good at this negotiation thing. You should've done it," Greg said as he threw his hands up.

"Now, now," Adriana replied. "You'll never get any better if you don't practice."

"This was just like Belfast in 1562," Greg replied. "I didn't make any headway."

"That beggar was deaf," Adriana said. "Besides, I knew this lady wasn't going to be receptive to accommodating us the moment I saw her. Too uptight."

The receptionist snorted.

"Then why did you let me go through that?" Greg asked.

"You needed the practice!" Adriana replied. "You probably need to attempt it more than once every five hundred years."

"It's only been like four hundred and fifty. No need to overexaggerate," Greg replied. "So, back to the original plan then."

Greg looked at the ginger haired man sitting on the couch.

"What about him?" Greg asked.

"He's Doctor Furnstein's next appointment," the receptionist answered.

Greg frowned at the receptionist. "I wasn't talking to you."

The receptionist opened her mouth to reply, but then just shook her head. She had to deal with all sorts coming through the door.

"He seems nice," Adriana said. "Pretty sure he'll go over the edge on his own within the next two years."

"Now who's acting like a therapist?" Greg scoffed. "Well, you'll have to take care of him."

Adriana walked over to the man. "Sorry, sweetie," she said as she pulled on some gloves and a roll of duct tape. "We're going to have to tie you up for a little while."

She punched the man in the jaw and his eyes rolled up in the back of his head as he fell to the floor.

"You leave him—" the receptionist started to say until Greg socked her across the jaw and she fell to the floor unconscious as well.

"Kid had a glass jaw," Adriana said and she rolled him onto his back, wrapped his wrists together in front, put tape over his mouth and secured his legs to a coffee table leg.

"Why'd you tape his hands in front and not behind?" Greg asked as he dragged the receptionist over next to the man.

"So he could fidget when he wakes up," Adriana said. "I'm not a monster."

They left the receptionist mostly free, but taped her mouth shut. She started to moan as she regained consciousness. Adriana stepped in front of Greg.

"Okay, you're gonna have to do the thing before I let her go," Adriana said.

"Oh, right," Greg said and punched Adriana in the jaw. She crumpled to the ground.

A few moments later, screams punctured the calm elevator music in the office as the good doctor killed his existing patient. There was the sound of something being dragged and then some doors closing. A few moments later, the inner office door opened.

Doctor Furnstein, a middle aged man who was going prematurely bald, poked his head out. His right hand holding the door open had some blood on it, leaving a little smear on the edge of the door.

"Okay, other patient is stashed in the armoire. Why this doctor has an armoire in his office I'll never know, but there it is."

The doctor walked over to the receptionist desk and grabbed a letter opener. The doctor walked over and kneeled down next to the receptionist and was about to stab her when Greg caught his arm.

"Wait, you think the doctor should rape her first?" Greg asked.

The doctor paused and looked thoughtful for a moment.

"Well, it turns out he's already banging her—sordid little affair too. Kind of be a waste of time and could put motive into doubt," the doctor replied.

"Mmm, still, heat of passion murder, so should be fairly messy. Let me drag Adriana into the office, then have at it," Greg said.

Greg dragged the unconscious Adriana into the office and laid her next to the recliner. He sat down in the recliner as he listened to the receptionist's muffled screams and then dying gurgle as the doctor dispatched her. After a few minutes, the doctor walked in and closed the door behind him. He sat down in the easy chair opposite the recliner.

"Eh, you probably should wash up," Greg said as he pointed to the doctor's hands and clothes.

The doctor looked down at his now crimson hands and blood stained clothes. He stood up and walked over to the private bathroom, stripped off the clothing and used some paper towels to wipe down the shoes. He left the bloody clothes in the bathroom and walked over to the armoire, carefully opened it up so only the former patient's arm fell out, and retrieved a new set of clothes.

"Well, now it makes sense," the doctor said. He tossed the clothes onto the easy chair and pushed the arm back into the armoire as he closed it. He quickly got dressed and sat back down.

"Now?" the doctor asked. Greg looked around the office and noticed a large paperweight on the desk behind the doctor was coated with blood. It dripped down the edge of the desk onto the floor.

"Should be fine. How did you keep the blood off the couch?" Greg responded.

"Oh, there was a throw on the couch behind the patient. I just angled the blows so most of the spatter would be on that. It's in the armoire too."

"Cool." Greg nodded and the doctor's head fell forward. He caught himself before falling to the ground and sat up, blinking rapidly.

Adriana suddenly sat up and stretched. She rubbed her jaw.

"Nice hook," she said to Greg.

"Thank you," Greg nodded.

The doctor looked at them both.

"Who are you?" he asked.

"Your four o'clock appointment," Greg said. "I'm Hades and this is Sphincter." Greg pointed at Adriana who was just getting up off the floor.

"Those are unusual names," the doctor said.

"Well," Adriana said. "They're more nicknames really, pet names if you like."

"Our actual names are unpronounceable in the human tongue, but my name is something like—" Greg emitted an earsplitting scream and guttural howl. The doctor ducked his head and covered his ears.

"That's hideous!" the doctor screamed. Greg and Adriana look at each other with knowing smiles. "What parents would name their kids that?"

"Parents?" Adriana asked. "Oh, you mean the bodies."

"I prefer to call them skin sacks," Greg said.

"What?" the doctor asked as he shook his head to clear his ears.

"So, the skin sacks then. I'm Greg Druzen and this is Adriana Gonzales," Greg said as he pointed to Adriana.

"It's Gonsalves," Adriana said and put her hands on her hips. "I keep telling you."

"Well, you think maybe you could pick a skin sack with an easier name to remember?" Greg said.

"You *know* this isn't easy!" Adriana hissed. "All the corruptive factors need to be in perfect balance! You're just being an ass."

The doctor looked at them with a blank stare. Greg and Adriana looked at him and smiled.

"Sorry," Adriana said. "We shouldn't be talking shop on your time."

"Do you need couples counseling?"

Adriana and Greg looked at each other and frowned. They shook their heads.

"No, I don't think so," Greg said. "Sphincter here thought we might need to see a professional about a professional concern."

"Sphincter?" the doctor asked. He looked at Greg. "And Hades? Why are those your nicknames?"

"Oh," Greg said holding up his hand to Adriana. "Let me explain. When we do a haunting or possession or whatever, I prefer the common theatrics of brimstone, you know the pure sulphur smell, but Sphincter prefers adding a bit of methane and carbon dioxide to the mix, getting more of an earthy, fecal flavor to the smell. Should we demonstrate?"

The doctor held up his hands quickly.

"No, no, that's okay!" He put his hands in his lap. "Look, I'm sure I don't remember booking an appointment with you two. I'll just get with Rebecca and get you referred to another psychiatrist."

"Your receptionist?" Greg looked at Adriana. "You know, I didn't even ask her name. Seems kind of rude of me."

"Probably doesn't matter if it's not a long-term relationship," Adriana replied. "She didn't offer it and she didn't stand up when we entered. I think she's the rude one."

Greg nodded and returned his attention to the doctor.

"You kind of gave her the day off. The night too, if you know what I mean, you sly dog," Greg said as he winked at the doctor.

"And I don't remember Mister Bower leaving," the doctor continued, pointedly ignoring Greg's insinuation.

"Oh, you ended his appointment early," Adriana said. "Of course, you don't remember that now, but you will before we leave. I promise."

"I still think you should leave," the doctor said as he stood up.

Adriana pulled a gun from her purse and pointed it at the doctor.

"Now doctor, shooting you isn't part of the plan, but I can easily vary from the plan if we get too much trouble from you." Adriana smiled sweetly.

Doctor Furnstein sat back down and set his hands in his lap with a sigh. "Okay, what do you want?"

"So," Greg said as he leaned forward. "On the Doctor Hank show, you said you were an expert on addiction."

"Sure, that's the main focus of my practice, but you two are leaning a bit more toward schizophrenia or a multiple personality diagnosis, rolled in with some kind of psychopathy, if you don't mind me saying," he replied eyeing the gun Adriana casually waved about.

"Well, we know about that—kind of a baseline for someone in our line of work, really," Adriana replied. "Sorry about the gun. Just trying to keep things simple, Doc." Adriana put the gun away.

"Okay," Doctor Furnstein said as he wiped at the sweat forming on his brow. It made a streak through the flecks of blood there. "You said you were here about addiction. Why do you think you may have a problem... with addiction."

"Well," Greg started as he sat back on the couch and stretched out his arms on the back. "Over the last twenty years, we've taken a fancy to putting a wager on the outcome of our work."

"Twenty-five," Adriana corrected.

"Really?" Greg sat forward. "Has it been twenty-five? Maybe we do have a problem. Times flies and I never realized."

Doctor Furnstein looked from Adriana to Greg and back. "You two can't be in your thirties even—how can you have been working at anything for twenty-five years?"

"What?" Greg asked. He thought for a moment and then grinned. "Oh yeah, the skin sacks. Yeah, they're just barely twenty-five years old. We've only been in them for about a week."

"You're mad," Doctor Furnstein whispered.

"No, I'm not upset at all!" Greg grinned. "I think this is going splendidly."

"I think he means insane," Adriana said.

"Oh, yeah, by human standards, absolutely. By demonic standards, we're really pretty average," Greg said as he shrugged his shoulders.

"Speak for yourself," Adriana sneered. "I'm above average!"

"I should've stuck with social work," Doctor Furnstein moaned.

"Oh no, we need your help with this possible addiction. We're concerned it might take over and affect our job performance," Greg said.

"I see." Doctor Furnstein rubbed his eyes and cleared his throat. "So, tell me, how do you feel about your gambling?"

Adriana and Greg looked at each other and smiled. "It's fun," they said in unison.

"Do you think it has adversely affected your relationships or work performance, can you think of anything besides gambling or are you obsessed with it?"

"Oh, I don't think we've ever been closer, really," Adriana said. "We enjoy the competitive nature it adds to our jobs. Really it's enhanced the job, if anything."

"Absolutely," Greg said and nodded emphatically.

"Have you lied about your gambling to your friends, have you experienced guilt about your gambling or how you feel when gambling?"

"I haven't lied and don't really experience guilt," Greg said frowning. "What about you, Sphincter?"

"No, Hades, can't say any of that pertains to me either."

"Okay, finally, have you been able to cut down or stop your gambling compulsion?"

"Well, we haven't wagered on anything in the last six months until we could make our way here for an evaluation," Adriana said.

"Oh." Greg popped up from the couch. "And we held off on any wagering for the five k celebration!"

"Five k celebration?" Doctor Furnstein asked.

"Sure," Greg said. "We have been haunting and tempting humans for over five thousand years. Well, it's been five thousand and seven now. But we totally devoted that entire celebration to concentrating on delivering a record number of souls—what was it, like two months?"

"Thirteen weeks," Adriana said. "I'm really looking forward to the next one! With the advances in technology sure to put you under group control of the rich and powerful within the next fifty years, I think we can leverage that tech to corrupting a record number of souls simultaneously!"

"The ten k celebration is going to be off the chain!" Greg shouted.

Doctor Furnstein shook his head. "You guys aren't addicted. You could have looked this all up on the internet, you know."

Greg looked disgusted. "Ugh, no. That internet thing creeps me out. That whole thing with the cookies? I mean, who names something you can't eat a cookie? That Al Gore is one sick bastard!" Greg sat down with a shudder.

"Yeah, okay, so there's my official diagnosis. You're just standard run-of-the-mill psychopaths. No gambling addiction." Doctor Furnstein sat back in the chair and rubbed his face.

"Run-of-the-mill?" Adriana screwed up her face. "No need to be rude."

"Now, now, Sphincter," Greg said as he grabbed Adriana's arm and led her to the door. "The good doctor didn't mean anything by it. We should let him get back to his insanity plea, yeah?"

"I suppose," Adriana said and then brightened. "Hey, Doc, you think you could be the default psychiatrist for demons?"

"I'm not going to have time for this nonsense. Now please leave."

"Oh, you're going to have plenty of time," Adriana said. "Oh wait, that's right! You don't remember."

"Remember what?" Doctor Furnstein asked.

Adriana walked to his chair and touched him on his forehead. She licked the traces of blood off her fingers. "It'll come back to you now. See you in the asylum." Adriana blew Doctor Furnstein a kiss and joined Greg at the office door. Doctor Furnstein's eyes got wide as the memories flooded into his head.

Adriana and Greg closed the door as they heard him shriek "What?!"

They walked past a now awake ginger haired man staring at the bloody corpse of the receptionist laying next to him and struggling to push himself away from it.

"I think we pushed ginger there over the edge. Probably got him there two or three years faster that he would've otherwise. I love efficiency," Adriana said as she walked out the door with Greg.

Before the reception office door shut, they could hear a bloodcurdling "No!" come from Doctor Furnstein as he found his murdered patient in the armoire.

"You know, he really knows his stuff," Greg said. "I can't wait for Whale Puke to see him. I really think he can help him with his confidence problem."